Caressing
Lions

Cynthia J. Sebring

ISBN 978-1-0980-0193-3 (paperback)
ISBN 978-1-0980-0194-0 (digital)

Copyright © 2019 by Cynthia J. Sebring

All rights reserved. No part of this publication may be reproduced, distributed, or transmitted in any form or by any means, including photocopying, recording, or other electronic or mechanical methods without the prior written permission of the publisher. For permission requests, solicit the publisher via the address below.

Christian Faith Publishing, Inc.
832 Park Avenue
Meadville, PA 16335
www.christianfaithpublishing.com

Printed in the United States of America

This book is dedicated with deepest thanks to the following individuals who encouraged my creative ambitions:

Dr. Joseph Arias, professor of Theology,
Christendom College, Front Royal, VA

The late Dr. Burns Broadhead, former District Superintendent
of the Methodist Church, Schuylkill Haven, PA

Rich and Joyce Swingle, internationally
known actors and missionaries

Special eternal thanks to our redeemer, the
greatest teacher and storyteller of all time:

Jesus Christ, Son of God, Messiah, Savior, the Lion of Judah

"The wicked run away
when no one is chasing them,
but the godly are as bold as lions."

—Proverbs 28:1 (NLT)

CHAPTER 1

*T*rying to reconstruct life on your own terms without a preliminary sketch is like a block of stone trying to chisel itself into a masterpiece. When you forge ahead without the creativity, perspective, and foresight of a sculptor, you end up creating a convoluted mess, not a Michelangelo. Sometimes, the chance to unleash hidden talent and heartfelt ambition requires a complete break from the past. Fortunately, some adventuresome souls possess the gumption to do just that.

Propped up against a canvas backpack and sleeping bag, Cory sat inside a train car about ten feet away from the open doorway. The necessity of free, immediate transportation outweighed any desire for luxury in first-class seating. After some considerable effort, he had managed to pry open a loose crate to find straw used for packing material, which served as the only buffer between him and the cold metal floor. As the afternoon sun shone through the opening, his back stiffened from sitting in the same position for several hours. Slowly, he stood up behind some large crates and stretched, relieving his muscles from their cramped position. A moment later, he resumed his place on the floor to avoid detection. As Cory sat there, he thought about how his father had confronted him the night before.

"I am tired of you doing nothing, you lazy kid! You can't find a job! How can you possibly ever amount to anything? Just get out!"

That was Mr. Clay Parker, subtle as a wrecking ball and sometimes just as emotionally damaging. This so-called "family" was not a unit, merely three miserable residents who cohabitated.

Consequently, Cory felt ostracized and more like a boarder in a tenement than a son in a home.

In sharp contrast, Cory's mother, Lilly, tried to convince him to never leave. From Mrs. Parker's perspective, life was an endurance contest and only the well-prepared and determined survived. Although Cory felt victimized, he also felt sorry for his mother. He understood how it was hard for a parent to lose an only child to adulthood, to no longer feel needed; nevertheless, he knew he had to become independent. Not only his mother's strangling nature, but also the house itself, always smelling of disinfectant but never flowers, seemed to suffocate his sense of individuality and a longing for new horizons.

Cory knew there was no point in arguing with his parents about how he was treated. A medieval peasant pleading for better living conditions from a feudal lord would have stood a better chance at a positive outcome.

Although Cory initially resented the comments, he eventually concluded that Dad was right in one respect. It was time to get out. The truth of the matter was Cory had actually grown disgusted with himself, although he would have never dared reveal this to his parents. Such an act equated to waving a white flag in front of a dictator, a meaningless gesture guaranteed not to help the victim gain any ground, but rather to increase the likelihood of oppression.

The catch was how to proceed. His parents had spelled out the problems extensively but had not offered even one remote solution. At twenty-two, somehow, he needed to find his own way in the world. He had already decided he was not going to be homesick. There was nothing to miss with one exception: his German shepherd. Lately, Cory had loved being around that dog more than most people, probably because the dog knew how to listen.

Without sufficient funds, the cheapest and fastest way to get out of town was to hop a freight train. He had been lucky no one had seen him get onboard. He had cautiously climbed inside the train with the silence and stealth of an army officer on field maneuvers. So far, so good. If his luck held out, he could stay a day or two onboard without being seen. How strange he thought to spend so many years craving positive attention and now he sought invisibility, to remain as transparent as the air. Sitting behind piles of boxes and crates kept him out of sight. Several times that day, the freight engineer walked within a few feet of him without realizing it.

As the train left the station, gradually gaining speed, Cory felt the air blow through the car. He zipped up his red jacket, pulled it tighter around him, and shoved his gloved hands into his pockets. Since the train made relatively frequent stops to load and unload cargo, it would take many hours till the train arrived in Pennsylvania.

Trying to prepare for the trip as best he could, in his backpack, he carried a few handfuls of nonperishables in one of the compartments. In a zippered pocket on the inside of his jacket, he carried some cash in an envelope, $1,530, his life savings. At this point, he would have to survive on that till he found a job. Since Cory had no idea how long that would take, he was determined not to spend a dime unless absolutely necessary.

After the train pulled into the next station an hour later, about fifty yards away, he heard crates being taken off and doors slamming shut. About five minutes later, an engineer called out all was clear and the train slowly began inching its way forward. He had not been found out and nodded off. He awoke a few hours later and looked at the skyline. The exact location of the treelined horizon with its autumn leaves was as unknown as his impromptu plans for tomorrow. He rested his head back down on his backpack, took a candy bar out of his pocket, and ate it for lunch. No matter what obstacles he faced, even hunger, going home was not an option, not until he could face his parents as an independent adult, instead of a needy kid.

As the train picked up speed, he watched the trees and buildings fly by and he began to wonder if he had made the right decision to travel this way. He knew it was a gamble hopping a train: the Russian roulette of hobos and stowaways like himself. He had heard alarming stories of travelers being seriously injured, attacked by guard dogs, robbed, and even killed doing exactly the same thing he was, but he had made his choice. All he could do right now was hope for the best.

While traversing through a patch of countryside, Cory noticed a church with its tall, white steeple in the distance. Taking a sip of water, he thought about his resolution to leave the church. If God did exist, he could not possibly approve of followers whose prayers displayed all the fervor of frozen fish in a Yukon cache. Compassion and charity remained nothing more than abstract theological constructs which no one ever practiced.

When Cory announced he would not attend church anymore, his father became so angry he had punched the wall and his mother had wept. Oddly, no one asked Cory why he made this decision. That morning summed up the toxic environment in the house: perpetually reactionary and never even remotely logical.

He wondered if they were surprised at his abrupt departure. They shouldn't have been. After all, his father had told him to get lost and, much to Cory's surprise, his mother had not raised an objection. He imagined how quiet the house must be with no one to yell at.

Now he chose to focus on a fresh start. The rhythmic motion of the train, as it swayed from side to side combined with the steady clank of the wheels on each section of track, created a hypnotic effect, which eventually lulled him to sleep again. Hours later, he woke to the sounds of shouting.

"Hey, kid! What do you think you are doing? Get out of there!"

Cory sat upright, startled to see an engineer staring at him.

"Get out now, or I will throw you out!"

The man in uniform stood well over six feet in height. From the tone of his voice, he was in no mood for a debate. Obviously, there was no point in arguing with a train official. Nothing was worth going to jail or having his guts kicked in. Without a word, Cory got up, threw his backpack and sleeping bag on the ground, and jumped off the side of the train. A sign in the distance read "Cleveland."

An unforeseen shift in travel options would not deter him from his ultimate destination. He picked up his belongings and walked at a quick pace, heading for a main road to try and hitch a ride. Looking at the road signs, Cory headed off toward the east. He turned up the collar on his jacket. A breeze had increased and was blowing steadily.

After an hour of hitchhiking in vain along the interstate, Cory finally managed to thumb down a trucker. On the side of the vehicle in bold green letters was written "West Penn Trucking—We Haul It All." The tandem wheeled big rig slowed to a crawl pulling over onto the shoulder of the road while the air brakes hissed as if the tires were sighing with relief in anticipation of a long overdue hiatus from perpetual motion. A middle-aged man in a dark green jacket and jeans opened the passenger door with a broad smile.

Scaling up the side of the truck was akin to Alpine climbing, an ascent into the heavens in microcosm, requiring precision in footing and leverage, as well as intense concentration. Upon reaching the bottom of the open door, about nine feet up, the driver took hold of Cory's backpack and bed roll and placed them on the floor. With less of a burden on his back, Cory grabbed on to the outside handles and with one last burst of strength, hauled himself into the seat. The change in elevation produced the illusion that the ground was a mile below them.

"Hey there. Where you headed?"

"Pittsburgh."

The driver looked a bit disappointed.

"I'm afraid I'm not going quite that far. I'm dropping off my supplies at a grocery store in Titusville. That's a couple hours north of Pittsburgh. Maybe you can get another ride from there."

The man's tone was amiable and sanguine. It was almost as if he were doing himself a favor, instead of doing one for Cory.

"Sir, as long as I am headed in the general direction, I'll be fine," said Cory casually.

Confidence and fortitude had proven to be two sweet condiments to serve with goal setting.

Cory adjusted the seat back another six inches, fastened his seatbelt, and stretched out his legs. The passenger side offered an enormous amount of leg room. Over a dozen circular gauges lined the dashboard along with various dials and switches creating the sensation he was copiloting a plane.

The trucker leaned over, turned the radio dial to a country music station, and gradually accelerated as the engine roared to life and the truck pulled out onto the road. The driver seemed genuinely glad to have some company.

"Have you ever been around the Titusville area before?"

"No, can't say that I have."

"The first oil well in the United States was drilled there. Most people think oil wells were first drilled in Texas or Oklahoma, but actually, it was Pennsylvania. It's a nice, small town. Good place to raise a family," explained the driver.

As they headed down the highway, Cory noticed several BMWs and SUVs pass them. He longed to get a car of his own, but something affordable. He didn't have the money for a vehicle of that quality.

"So have you had a chance to travel much in the US?" the man asked cordially.

"No, I have mostly seen the Chicago area. That's where I'm from. I'm heading east to find a job."

"What kind of work are you looking for?"

"Anything I can at this point. At the moment, I cannot afford to be particular. I'll have to start at the bottom and work my way up, but everyone has to do that, I guess."

As he looked out the windshield, Cory felt grateful he was no longer trying to hitch a ride. The wind had gained momentum and storm clouds had gathered on the horizon, thunderheads, swirling masses towering over the skyline, and they were driving straight toward them.

The driver made a slight adjustment to the rearview mirror.

"You might have to start at the bottom, but don't think small. Think about opportunities and ways to use your own potential. That way you will probably end up with more fulfilling work."

"How long have you been a truck driver?" Cory asked.

"Thirty years. Good job. Steady pay. Good benefits. The only drawback is it keeps me away from my family too often. I have a son about your age. He works in Pittsburgh. He majored in business administration and completed an internship at a bank. That experience helped him get his job as a director of finance."

Listening to the man talk, all of a sudden, Cory regretted not attending college when he had the chance. He earned qualifying grades for most universities. In fact, he even won a national award through the school science fair for a project on instinctive behaviors of wild cats in Africa.

On top of that, his parents even offered to cover his college tuition. Unfortunately, he lacked motivation to apply his aptitude as a teenager. Cory wondered why he had not seen that offer as an opportunity for success. Shortsightedness had generated its own negative consequences.

"It sounds like you are very proud of your son."

As large drops of rain began to splatter on the windshield, the man adjusted his speed and turned on the headlights and wiper blades. Feeling a sudden drop in temperature, the trucker reached over and turned on the heat. The blast of hot air circulated straight out and upward and immediately started to relax Cory's aching muscles. Cory leaned his head a little further back into the headrest.

The trucker smiled broadly. "You bet I am proud of my son. He's a wonderful young man. He's a hard worker, responsible, and he's also a good person. He's always thinking about other people, not just how to make another dollar."

The driver paused and looked pensive for a moment.

"It wasn't easy for him growing up. His mom died when he was three. It was a tough time for both of us, but we decided a long time ago it's better to move forward."

Although he wasn't sure why, Cory suddenly realized how fortunate he had been to grow up with both parents, even if he found it problematical to get along with them.

"I'm sorry to hear about your wife, sir. I can't imagine what that must be like, but I agree with you. The best thing anyone can do is move forward. Where and how are the real questions."

As they drove into the pouring rain, the radio announcer introduced the song "I'll Fly Away" and the driver smiled and began singing the gospel tune quietly to himself about flying away to heaven.

Ironically, the wiper blades moved back and forth with the same tempo as the music.

"So what do you think happens when you die?"

For a second, Cory lost his breath. He stared at the man, stunned and speechless. The question made the same impact as the day he got hit in the head with a snowball, while walking to school. It came at him out of nowhere, jarring him back to reality, causing his daydreams to disintegrate.

By this time, the rain was coming down in a blinding torrent. At first, Cory pondered how the driver could see the road at all, but he had no trouble managing the vehicle. No doubt years of experience driving great distances in all kinds of weather had prepared him for anything. Cory also noted that the truck was equipped with tremendously powerful headlights. If the trucker ever needed to, he could no doubt maneuver his way through a Chicago blizzard.

To compensate for the almost deafening sound of the rain, Cory said in a loud voice, "I don't know. Maybe we just sort of disappear when we leave this world. Maybe there isn't anything."

The trucker gave Cory a long, stern look.

"My son once thought like you do, but one experience changed all that in an instant. When he was sixteen, a drunk driver crashed into his car. My son was blessed that the way he took the impact didn't break bones, but it left him with a concussion. He spent several days in the hospital. During that time, he had a vision of heaven and the Lord told him about some changes he needed to make in his life. He acted like a different person afterward. That's when he started sincerely caring about others. He also began showing me a ton of respect."

He looked at Cory again. "Believe me, there's more to life than this biological world we live in. Any doubts I ever had about that vanished when my son described to me what he saw in heaven."

Cory didn't know what to make of the young man's near-death experience. He wanted to know exactly what the man encountered; on the other hand, he was far too unnerved to ask. This life was arduous enough to get through. If there is another life after this one, how do you plan for that?

Trying to give a simple, innocuous response, Cory replied, "Well, whatever the truth is, I hope I figure it out. If there is a heaven, I'd like to see it someday."

"It exists and you can see it, but the only way to do that is to get to know God, the one who owns the real estate. After all, that's his home that you would be moving into. No one wants to live with a total stranger."

"That makes sense."

The trucker continued. "God will accept you, if you accept him as your means of salvation. Jesus paid for your sins. He wants everyone to acknowledge that and live accordingly."

"What do you mean by 'acknowledge that'? If he died for my sins, then I'm automatically covered, right?"

The trucker shook his head. "No. This is not like being added on to your father's auto insurance policy when you turned sixteen. Look at it this way. What Jesus is offering is sort of like a marriage proposal. There is no wedding unless the other person says 'Yes.' If the potential bride ignores the question, there is no wedding. Likewise, if you don't say 'Yes' to Jesus and live accordingly, there is no salvation."

"That part makes sense, except, well, why do I need saving? After all, I wouldn't call myself a sinner. I'm not a bad person. Isn't hell just for people like Jesse James and Hitler? I don't rob banks or kill people. I don't steal cars. I'm not some terrorist. I have no intentions of dropping a bomb or flying a plane into a building."

The driver grinned. "No, of course not, but committing one sin, even something you think of as insignificant, makes you guilty of breaking all of them. Sin cannot be taken lightly. You might seem good by your own standards, but you are a sinner by God's standards. Let me put it to you this way. Ever been jealous of someone else's success? Ever condemned another person's actions or words so you felt more powerful, the center of attention? Have you ever experienced a fit of rage or told a lie? Ever stolen something or thought about it? Have you ever openly disrespected or ignored someone in authority like your parents or a teacher?"

Cory ran through the list of questions in his mind. Unknowingly, to a large extent, the truck driver had just described his daily life under his parents' roof and his attitude toward a few belligerent neighbors.

"Yes, actually, I guess at some point I have done all those things."

As he spoke, guilt began to settle down upon him like a dense fog over a bay. He could not ignore it. Guilt permeated him, saturated him, forcing him to examine his own actions. Silently, he apologized to God for his past and noted the subtle change in his physical countenance. It was as if his mind were expelling toxins and he began to think more clearly. To his amazement, Cory realized that his own thoughts had become more shocking to him than the driver's initial question.

Cory looked at the driver for a moment with admiration. Unlike his parents, here was someone who put his beliefs into practice. After all, the trucker had reached out in compassion, instead of deciding he was too busy to stop. No one else had bothered to offer him a lift.

"I'm glad you can be honest with yourself. Those are examples of sins. Of course, they aren't as serious as murder or armed robbery, but nevertheless, it was wrong to do those things. Jesus covers those sins if you ask him to. He paid for them."

"Why would some little sin matter? It almost sounds like God is too particular."

"Okay. Here's a scenario. Let's say I'm driving down the road and a cop pulls me over for running a red light. Would it do any good to say, 'But, Officer, I didn't kill a pedestrian. I didn't hit another car so what difference does it make if I ran a red light? Aren't you being too particular?' Do you really think he is going to buy that as a good excuse?" asked the driver.

Cory shook his head. "No, I suppose not. I see what you mean."

"That is why we need Jesus to cover our sins. Even something small not just major transgressions. God is perfect and the only way we can likewise be faultless is through the atonement of Jesus."

"But what if I want to pay for my own sins? Why do I need somebody else to do that?"

The trucker looked at him sideways as if Cory had lost his mind.

"I don't think you realize what you are asking. If you want to spend eternity in hell fire paying for your own sins, that is an option, but why would you want to? Why would you want to suffer, experience separation from eternal love, and throw away the destiny God has planned for you? Where is the logic in that?"

"I guess, if Jesus is real, it would be best to take him up on his offer."

The trucker smiled. "He's real and you would be very wise to take him up on his offer. You aren't going to get a better one."

As the rain diminished, the trucker adjusted the speed of the wiper blades. Patches of blue began to appear in the late afternoon sky. They drove down the highway for a few minutes in silence, while Cory examined a state map to figure out the location of Titusville in juxtaposition to neighboring towns and the city of Pittsburgh.

"What kind of work does your son do?" asked Cory out of idle curiosity.

"He handles a major portion of the budget at the Pittsburgh Zoo, but his favorite part of the job is working with animals."

"I wonder what it would be like to work with animals all day long instead of office staff, confined to a desk for most of the day. Since I'm heading for Pittsburgh, maybe I'll have a chance to meet him. What's his name?"

"Daniel Franklin. He has worked there for about six years."

"Maybe I can run into him sometime when I get to Pittsburgh. I can say 'hello' for you and tell him how we met."

"Good idea. He probably would enjoy a good story like that. He's quite sociable."

By the time they pulled into Titusville, the rain had stopped and the sun hung low on the horizon. The trucker turned down a side street and into a parking lot behind a grocery store.

"Well, young man, that's the end of the ride. I've got some granola bars in the glove compartment. Go ahead and take some with you."

Cory reached in and took two bars out of a box. "Thanks."

"Nice talking with you. All the best. God bless you."

Cory climbed back down to earth one cautious step at a time.

"Thanks, Mr. Franklin. I really appreciated the lift. I'll say 'hi' to your son, if I see him."

Cory watched as the driver got out, opened the sides of the truck, and began unloading produce with the help of some store employees. Cory waved goodbye again. The driver eyed the young man a moment, smiled, and returned the wave.

Cory headed for the main road.

He was alone again.

CHAPTER 2

𝒞ory could see the downtown area with restaurants, shops, a hospital, and gas stations. Having looked at a map, he knew approximately where he was headed. As he walked, he kept replaying the dialogue with the trucker, or the man he knew now as Mr. Franklin, over and over like a closed-circuit film. He began deciphering which parts of their talk he agreed with and what ideas still left him mystified. The entire conversation had piqued his interest.

As the evening air grew colder, Cory tried to hitch a ride as he reflected more on the driver's words. His son had seen heaven and that had changed everything. Cory had still not fully recuperated from the thought of someone actually encountering the supernatural. He wondered for a moment what he would do if he saw God. Pray? Faint? Ask for mercy? Stand there speechless?

As several cars passed him, Cory thought about the man's generosity and sincerity in his faith. He wished that he possessed in his life what Mr. Franklin had: certainty about the next life and a sense of purpose in this one. He also wished he could talk with his own father as easily as he had that truck driver.

After thirty minutes, he had not managed to get another ride, so Cory began to wonder where he could spend the night. The few motels he had passed displayed a red "No Vacancy" sign flashing out front. Since it was Columbus Day weekend, tourists were probably visiting relatives or in transit to recreational areas like Cooks Forest or Lake Erie in an attempt to fit in one more excursion before heading back to work.

After some careful consideration, he decided rather than stay in town, he might be safer heading out into the woods, where he wouldn't be seen. After all, he didn't want to get picked up by the police for vagrancy or robbed by some deranged mugger who might find him sleeping on a park bench.

Heading up a hill, outside of town, he began trekking through a forested area. Taking out his flashlight, Cory guarded his steps and stayed on a path he discovered, wondering where it might lead. A full moon that evening provided some additional light. The unexpected, wooded acreage almost seemed out of place, an abrupt transition from city life, an oasis. When he had walked to the point where he no longer could see the lights of downtown, he figured that was probably far enough and headed for a small clearing to unroll his sleeping bag. As he was about to settle down for the night, he made out the side of a log cabin nestled amongst some trees. Walking along the path leading to the structure, he found a sign with an arrow pointing to the building that read: "Cabins for rent by the day, week, or month."

Overjoyed at his unanticipated find, he approached the cabin and knocked on the heavy, wooden door. No one answered. The place was dark. He hesitated about trying to enter but decided the night air would be too much for him, making the option of sleeping indoors all the more favorable. He tried moving the door handle and discovered to his delight it was unlocked. Turning on the light and glancing about the room, he noted the cabin looked ready for guests. The interior appeared immaculate with everything in its place.

Although somewhat against his better judgment, Cory decided staying here, even though he had not officially signed in anywhere, was preferable to facing potential weather hazards. While riding in the truck, he heard the radio announcer mention another rainstorm was heading through the area later on that night with a greater drop in temperature than the night before.

After closing the front door securely, he walked to the massive, stone fireplace, and set his backpack and sleeping bag down. Spying some firewood by the hearth, he arranged some logs and got a blaze going in a few minutes, hoping that the proprietor would not mind that he was spending the night. He would have to figure out how to pay for the rental sometime tomorrow.

Feeling quite hungry, Cory opened his backpack and took out a metal spoon, a can opener, and a can of baked beans. Aside from the candy bar for lunch, he hadn't eaten all day, so regardless of its simplicity, the meal would feel satisfying. He sat down cross-legged by the fire on an oval, wool rug and began to eat the beans cold, right out of the can. Anything tasted good on an empty stomach. After a few minutes, the warmth from the flames took the chill out of his back.

Looking around the cabin, he noticed a kitchen off to one side with a counter lined with a few appliances and supplies, a single bed, neatly made with a thick quilt, a nightstand and lamp, and a wide leather sofa, large enough to sleep on easily, and a matching leather chair in front of the stone fireplace with a thick oak mantel running its entire length. Red and white checkered drapes hung at the windows. Along the walls, Cory noticed several framed posters and photos with scenic views of national parks that he recognized from magazines and vacations out west. The chandelier was made out of deer antlers. This place wasn't a plush resort, but compared to sleeping on the hard ground, exposed to the cold night air, it felt like a mansion.

About the time Cory had eaten half the beans, the front door opened with a loud bang and a tall man in a leather jacket, a green shirt, jeans, and hiking boots stepped in carrying a rifle. The man turned, saw Cory, and pointed his rifle right at him.

"What are you doing here? You a thief?"

Panic-stricken, Cory instinctively raised both hands in the air. From the man's abrupt entrance, obviously he knew in advance someone was inside. Cory quickly deduced he must have smelled the smoke rising from the chimney and seen the lights shining through the thin, closed drapes.

Gasping for some air, trying not to hyperventilate, Cory replied, "No, sir. I didn't come to steal. I came in to get warm. I even brought my own food. I didn't take yours. Honest."

The man looked down at the can of beans at Cory's feet. Obviously, he had not raided the refrigerator.

"How did you get in here? Did you break my lock?"

"No, sir. I didn't break anything. The door was unlocked. Honest."

The man turned sideways, examined the door latch and hinges, noticed they were intact, and then shut the door. He was still holding the rifle.

"Sir, if this is the place you're renting, I'm sorry to intrude. I didn't make a reservation because I didn't know these cabins existed. I just found this place about ten minutes ago by accident. The place looked so clean I didn't think anyone was staying here. I would have phoned someone, but there's no number on the sign out front. It was an honest mistake, sir."

Seeing Cory's hands still raised in the air, the man leaned the gun up against the wall. Slowly, Cory lowered his hands, but his heart continued to pound fiercely like a demolition crew was slamming into his chest full force with a sledgehammer.

Glancing around the room, the man noted none of his personal belongings had been moved. Everything remained in its proper place. The man slowly moved closer to Cory, sat down in the chair by the fireplace, and looked at the unexpected visitor. His instincts told him this was definitely no thief, just a vacationer or maybe a young man trekking across America.

To Cory's surprise, the man smiled at him and leaned back in the chair. Intuitively, the man sensed this young man exuded an innocence like he had never been in serious trouble before in his entire life. He discerned the young man had been telling him the truth from the beginning.

"I'm sorry. I wasn't trying to scare you to death, but I had to be sure. Residents in these parts have been robbed. I guess I left the door unlocked inadvertently. That was careless of me."

He paused and looked up at the ceiling.

"You know something, no number on that sign equates to poor advertising, doesn't it? That needs to change. Next time I'll hire a professional instead of trying to do it myself," said the man calmly.

Leaning slightly forward, the man extended his hand in greeting.

"My name's Paul Jamison. I own these cabins and this particular one is my home. All the other cabins are booked this weekend, so I can't put you up somewhere else, but there's no need to pay me. You can stay here, if you need to. What brings you this way?"

Cory gladly accepted the handshake. His heart was finally beginning to calm down. For a moment, he believed he would never see dawn again, let alone Pittsburgh.

"I'm trying to relocate. In the process, I just ended up here; that's all."

Paul studied the young man for a moment. Cory looked exhausted. His jacket and jeans were stained and his shoes were dirty. Paul wondered what this guy had been eating besides beans.

"What's your name?"

"Cory. Cory Parker."

"Well, Cory, it is nice to meet you. Where are you from?"

"Chicago. I plan on going to Pittsburgh to find work."

"Well, there are certainly plenty of job opportunities in Pittsburgh, but that's still quite a way from here."

Cory looked intently at Mr. Jamison. Noticing the lines in the man's face, Cory judged he was probably about fifty. Sitting relaxed in the chair, without his rifle, somehow Mr. Jamison displayed an atmosphere of peace about him as if somehow all was right with the world or at least, all was right with his world.

"It's going to get colder tonight. You can put another log on the fire if you like."

Without hesitating, Cory grabbed a log and placed it on top of the others. The dry wood caught instantaneously and the fire burned brightly. Since the cabin stood so far away from the noise of the town, the only sounds were the snapping and crackling of the logs until Mr. Jamison spoke.

"Are you hungry? Do you want something more to eat?"

In actuality, Cory was famished, but he did not want to impose and perhaps jeopardize his night's lodgings.

"No, sir. I am fine for now. Thank you. I was noticing your posters. I like the one of Glacier National Park. I went hiking there one summer and rented a car so I could drive on Going-to-the-Sun Road. Very scenic and full of wildlife. I photographed a herd of mountain goats."

"Yes, that is a lovely area. My father and I vacationed there when I was fifteen. I'm glad you're interested in the outdoors. Too many young people these days want to spend their whole lives inside, staring at cell phones, television, and video games. I only have the one bed. You can sleep on the sofa if you want or on the rug closer to the fireplace. Take your pick. It's been a long day. I'm going to get some sleep."

"Thank you, sir. I really appreciate it. That's kind of you."

"You're quite welcome."

Cory was ready to pass out from relief. He could hardly believe this fortuitous encounter. A free night's lodging and someone to talk to. How often do things like this happen? He watched as Mr. Jamison bolted the front door, locked the rifle up in a cabinet, sat down on the edge of the bed, and took off his left boot.

On the wall, Cory saw a metal cross hanging on the pine paneling over the nightstand.

"Sir? Can I ask you something?" Paul nodded. "Do you believe in Jesus?"

Paul smiled. "Yes, I do. What about you? What do you believe?"

Cory thought for a moment.

"Well, I went to church as a kid, but then I told my parents I didn't want to go anymore. It seemed like a waste of time."

Leaning forward, Paul looked directly into Cory's dark eyes.

"Let me tell you something, young man. God is never a waste of time. It makes no sense to say you don't want to make time for God. That's like saying it's a waste of time to eat and breathe. Your soul needs God as much as your body needs food and oxygen. You remember that."

The sermon was over, short and to the point. This was the second time that day a total stranger had given him a lesson in faith.

Paul took off his other boot and pointed to a closet.

"There are some blankets and pillows in there. Help yourself."

After finishing his can of beans, Cory unrolled his sleeping bag on the sofa, took a pillow and a wool blanket from the closet, and fixed up a bed for himself.

"Thank you, sir. This is kind of you."

Cory crawled inside the sleeping bag with the soft, wool blanket directly on top of him. With the fire blazing away, he was quite comfortable.

"We'll talk more tomorrow. Good night."

The fire continued to burn brightly for a few more hours. The scent of smoke reminded Cory of a camping trip he had enjoyed with his father many years ago, a time when he and his dad had been on better terms.

The next morning, Cory awoke to the smell of bacon and pancakes. The aroma was delightfully intoxicating. Of course, anything was more appetizing than dining on another can of beans. Cory sat up and watched as the man flipped over two pancakes, browned the bottom side, and placed two plates on a small table beside the stove. A container of flour stood on the counter along with a flour sifter, a carton of eggs, a pint of blueberries, vanilla extract, and some butter. Obviously, Mr. Jamison had made the pancakes from scratch. As an added decorative touch, a glass vase filled with yellow and white daisies stood in the center of the table.

"Good morning, Mr. Jamison," said Cory filled with optimism about this new segment of his journey.

The man was wearing a blue sweater, cotton slacks, and tennis shoes. Sunlight shone in through the kitchen window, lighting up Mr. Jamison's hands as he finished cooking.

"It's okay for you to call me Paul. I don't mind. Come on over and get some breakfast."

Those words were like the gentle reverberations of a piano concerto drowning out the rumblings of Cory's stomach. Mr. Jamison set the plates of food on the table and sat across from Cory, who delighted in the idea of eating pancakes hot off the griddle.

As Cory stared at the food, ready to commence eating, Paul asked, "Would you like to say grace, or should I?"

Cory looked at him a moment, feeling rather embarrassed and shrugged his shoulders.

"I'm not sure what to say to God. At times, I wonder if he even exists."

Paul looked intently at Cory.

"He exists. In fact, he's here right now. There's no time like the present to pray. Just tell the Lord what you're thinking just like you would talk to a friend. That's all it is."

With ancient, parental criticisms still ringing in his ears, Cory hesitated. He began slowly.

"Hi, God. It's me, Cory. I just wanted to say thanks for the breakfast and for a place to sleep last night and thanks for letting me meet Paul. Amen."

In a reassuring tone, Paul said, "If you always keep those lines of communication open with God, you'll be much happier."

Feeling more relaxed, Cory reached for the butter and syrup. Anticipating the large, cold square of butter to melt and slide down the pancakes was like waiting for a glacier to move down the side of a mountain, but worth the wait. Cory loved the combined flavors of butter and syrup which he generously poured directly over the melting butter with precision timing. In a way, the stack of pancakes resembled a work of art. He cut through a section of pancake and ate it quickly. It was absolutely delicious.

After eating for a few minutes in silence, Cory said, "Paul. Thank you. This is absolutely fantastic. Believe it or not, this is actually my favorite breakfast."

"I'm glad to hear that."

He watched Cory cut through another section of the blueberry pancakes, adding more syrup.

"Are you planning on staying in the area or heading out today?"

"At this point, I plan on taking a bus to Pittsburgh and moving in with a friend. I'll need to contact him, but I know he won't mind letting me stay with him," said Cory, biting into a bacon strip.

It was now obvious to Paul that Cory was famished.

"Besides renting out cabins, do you do any other work in the area, Paul?"

"Yes, I'm an auto mechanic. I work at a Ford dealership in town."

"Eventually, I would like to get a medium sized car. Probably used. What would you recommend?" asked Cory.

"Personally, I like the Ford Fiesta. It's economical and not as expensive as some of the larger models."

"Do you enjoy your work?" asked Cory out of curiosity.

"Absolutely. I love cars and like working with people. I especially enjoy being around a satisfied customer."

Paul poured two glasses of orange juice, putting one in front of Cory, who drank half of it in seconds. As the coffee finished brewing, Paul got up and prepared a cup for each of them.

"There's more bacon on the other plate by the stove, if you want some."

"Thanks, Paul."

After fixing his coffee, Cory took a few sips and sighed.

"Paul, can I ask you something?"

"Sure."

"What's the best way to tell two people you don't want them interfering in your life?"

"Just be open and honest and tell them how you feel."

"What if they don't want to listen and make up excuses for their actions?"

"Explain how important it is that they listen. Tell them plainly you are not interested in excuses. Tell them you are an adult and capable of making your own decisions. If you mess up, you are willing to deal with the consequences," said Paul.

Cory sensed that Paul concluded that he was talking about a parental issue, but he neither probed further with questions nor did he pass judgement over Cory's situation.

"Perhaps you're right. The direct approach might work to resolve this. I need to be more emphatic and say exactly what I think," said Cory, thinking out loud.

Paul got up and put some of the dirty dishes in the sink and rejoined Cory at the table.

"Cory, do you know what a tent revival is?"

"I'm not sure. I think I might have heard about one once."

Paul offered Cory more coffee, which he gladly accepted. He took several sips from the cup and breathed deeply, relaxed and contented to feel warm on the inside as well. Paul also put the second plate of bacon on the table and Cory took two more strips.

"Well, Cory, a tent revival is a praise gathering held outside in an oversized tent. Anyone can come. It doesn't matter what denomination you are or even if you belong to a church. Locals and other folks from out of town come there to worship God, sing, pray, and enjoy each other's fellowship. I will be attending a tent revival in the area this afternoon around four o'clock. It's about a twenty-minute drive. You can join me if you like."

Despite the kind offer, a strong reluctance began mounting inside Cory. He wanted to tell the man he absolutely had no interest in attending a service, indoors or out. Nevertheless, he didn't want to sound rude or unappreciative after all the hospitality Mr. Jamison had offered.

With reservation, Cory replied, "Yes, sir. I guess I'd like to go and check it out."

"Good. I have to work today. You can hang out here, if you want. There's a TV inside that cabinet beside the fireplace over there. I also have a few dozen books and magazines you could look at. For lunch, I have cold cuts and cheese in the refrigerator as well as some leftover fried chicken and coleslaw. There's a hiking trail that starts just behind the house and leads down to a creek with a view of the hills, if you want to check that out. If you would like to wash your clothes, the washer and dryer are next to the bathroom. Get a hot shower too, if you like. There are clean towels in the bathroom cupboard. I'll leave an extra key here on the nightstand in case you go out for a walk. That way you can lock up when you go and still get back in. I will be home around three thirty."

Cory nodded and smiled. "Thank you. That sounds fine."

Looking at the dirty dishes, Cory said to Paul, "I'll clean this up. You go ahead and go to work."

As Cory began the process of washing the dishes and silverware, he tried to remember the last time he had willingly taken on a task as a labor of love. Noticing subtle, positive changes in himself gave him a sense of self-satisfaction.

CHAPTER 3

*I*n the afternoon, while driving to the revival meeting with Paul, Cory began to reflect on what he had gotten himself into. His church in Chicago was filled with almost nothing but members of the geriatric set waiting to die. He was usually so bored sitting in the pew that sometimes he thought he would die himself from old age waiting for the sermon to end. Nothing his pastor said grabbed his attention. In fact, it always sounded like the same message being recycled like yesterday's newspapers. Only the words were different.

To his surprise, as they pulled into the field to park, Cory saw a plethora of young adults, kids in their teens, and young mothers with children, as well as some elderly men and women. Everyone was smiling and greeting one another. Cory reflected that he had never seen his own family that exuberant over anything, not even over Christmas festivities. Holidays always seemed like one more day on the calendar when his parents could vent their frustrations, instead of an occasion to celebrate.

On a hillside, a group of men were bringing folding chairs into an enormous white tent similar to the one used at his cousin's wedding reception. As Cory surveyed the area, he watched several young men carrying musical instruments and realized that this evening "church" was going to take on a whole new dimension.

Paul carried a large crockpot filled with bratwurst and sauerkraut for a potluck dinner following the service. Coming up from the other side, Cory could see throngs of people making their way toward the tent.

As he walked inside, he was amazed to see so many individuals already seated. Several musicians were tuning guitars, testing amplifiers, and setting up mike stands. As Cory sat down next to Paul, a group of young men walked by him, stopping to shake his hand.

"Hey, glad you could come. There's a dance afterward with dinner and refreshments in the adjacent tent, if you want to come and meet some people," they said cheerfully.

As Cory became more attuned to his surroundings, he noticed a few details of this environment with greater interest and awareness: the smell of freshly mowed grass, the autumn breeze that caused the sides of the tent to snap gently back and forth, and the amiable chatter of several hundred voices.

Finally, the band began playing a song: *Jesus Lifted Me*. Everyone stood and joined in clapping and singing. The energy in the room was contagious. It was like watching an electrical current turn on a thousand lights at the same time. After several more musical numbers, a man stepped to the front and gestured for everyone to be seated.

Silence enveloped the space like a tangible substance wrapping around the group, uniting them in the spirit of joyous anticipation. The man, tall with dark hair, looked about thirty years old. He wore jeans, a plain white T-shirt, and a denim jacket. His mannerisms were as casual as his dress. Strolling to the center of the stage, he picked up the microphone with one hand, while holding a Bible in the other.

"Brothers and sisters," he said boldly into the microphone, "we have come here tonight to worship the Lord, to praise the Almighty, to adore the King of Kings. He has been seeking us, since the day we were born. Tonight, we are going to seek him."

With an authoritative voice, he almost sounded like a commander addressing his troops, yet the tone was counterbalanced with compassion. He loved these people.

"God is with us as he promised: 'When two or more of you are gathered in my name, I shall be in the midst of you.'"

Aside from a lone "Amen" from the back row, there was silence. Whoever this man was, he commanded a great deal of respect. With the same boldness, the preacher began again.

"Brothers and sisters, I am Brother Neil from Tennessee and I consider it a privilege to worship with you tonight in the beautiful state of Pennsylvania. I have heard this glorious state referred to as 'God's country.' It is my prayer, it is my vision that all of America will one day be God's country."

He bowed his head and with his right arm stretched up toward heaven, he prayed, "Lord, I thank you that you have brought so many to this meeting. It is by your strength, your prompting, that believers and nonbelievers seek you. I pray, dear Lord, that these men and women will not leave here tonight without knowing who you truly are and who they are as your children made in your image. May your words go forth. Be with us and bless us, in Jesus's mighty name. Amen. Hallelujah."

With his right arm still raised in the air, the preacher gazed up at the roof of the tent as if expecting the canvas to rent in two, the heavens to open, and a host of angels to descend at any moment. Slowly, he lowered his arm and looked out at the faces in the congregation. His dark eyes flashed as if somehow, they were generating their own lightning.

"Brothers and sisters, tonight I want to talk with you about God's forgiveness. The good Lord said in Matthew 6:14, 'If you forgive others when they sin against you, your heavenly Father will also forgive you.' Forgive and you shall be forgiven. No matter what sins you have committed, you are covered by Christ's blood, if you believe in his holy atonement and repent of your sins. Can I hear an amen?"

Immediately, the tent almost shook with a resounding chorus of "Amen!" and just as quickly became silent once more. The gathering regained its complete composure, absolute stillness. In fact, for a moment, it was so quiet Cory could almost swear he could hear his blood circulating.

The preacher continued. "When we truly forgive others, we set aside our differences. We allow God to transform our emotions and renew our minds."

The preacher opened up his Bible.

"It says in Romans 12:2, 'Do not conform to the pattern of this world but be transformed by the renewing of your mind.' When our minds are renewed, we can more fully live for Christ."

He turned the pages of the Bible.

"Ephesians 4:31–32 says, 'Get rid of all bitterness, rage, anger, brawling, and slander along with every form of malice. Be kind and compassionate one to another, forgiving each other just as in Christ God forgave you.'"

As Cory listened, he wished someone would read those verses to his parents. They had sat through a number of sermons on forgiveness and yet that message had never penetrated their stubborn minds. At that moment, Cory realized he was guilty of the same thing, no desire to forgive.

The pastor walked toward the front of the platform.

"Think on this amazing love, brothers and sisters. Jesus died for the sins of those who have not even been born yet. In his infinite wisdom, he knew what sins needed to be covered. He knew how to apply his glorious power to each individual soul so each person would have a chance to see the light of heaven. God is not a respecter of persons. He does not show partiality. He died, yes, he died for all sinners."

He began to walk slowly back and forth in front of the congregation.

"If you want forgiveness, if you want to be part of the bride of Christ, you need to get a divorce from the world and its materialism, its idols, its vanities. Get a divorce from toxic pride and lethal resentments and forgive those who have wronged you. In turn, God will forgive your sins."

Cory reflected on the trucker's statement about the way accepting Christ was like saying "Yes" to a marriage proposal. It felt reassuring to hear the same message again. The preacher paused in the center of the stage and then walked to the right side of the platform.

"If you have a stony heart, if you have little to no room for the love of God and neighbor so you can receive God's forgiveness, I say to you tonight, you are in need of a heart transplant. The good news is that God is a great physician. Let God throw away that stone and give you a heart that beats for Him. When you have that heart, brothers and sisters, you can embrace God's forgiveness and in turn forgive others."

He paused and looked at a few individuals seated in the front row.

"You need to look at your heart and see if you have built up any walls between you and God. If you have, you must tear those walls down. Tear them down, brothers and sisters! Be like Joshua! March around those walls, cry out to God, and you will see those walls fall down. Walls of unforgiveness. Walls of selfishness. When you do, you will know the presence of God. You will be forgiven and you will experience the power to forgive. Can I hear an Amen somebody?"

Once again, a thunderous resound of "Amen" filled the tent. The congregation was entranced by the preacher's energy and the faith he placed in God and holy scripture.

"If you want to be close to Jesus, you need to know who he is. He is the savior of the repentant. He is God's own Son. He is divine countenance in human form. He possesses more power and wealth than any human can fathom and yet, in him there is no corruption. He heals addictions. He is a friend, a brother, a high priest, an intercessor, and the sacrifice for our sins. He is the Lamb of God and the Lion of Judah. Do you know him? Do you want to? Can I get an Amen from somebody?"

Another shout of "Amen" rocked the tent.

"If this message of forgiveness and salvation is new to any of you out there, let me say this. God is real. He is alive and he is interested in you personally. He cares about every aspect of your life. He knows your name and he calls you by name. He calls you this evening to heal your soul and body."

Cory stared in astonishment. God knew him and cared about him personally? Up until three days ago, Cory's best notion of God consisted of some being on the other end of the cosmos who created everything and then took a permanent vacation like an absentee landlord who never concerned himself with the condition of the house, leaving the tenants to fend for themselves. At home, most of the time Cory felt closer to the mailman than he did his own parents, let alone God. Now, someone claimed God knew him by name, knew everything about him. Could this be possible?

The preacher prayed silently a moment and continued, "Someone here tonight has struggled with cigarettes. God says he has been healing you of that addiction for the past several days."

Something in the atmosphere shifted. How often had he tried to give up smoking? He had lost count. Cory suddenly had the revelation that he had not smoked a cigarette for the past three days, nor had he even desired to do so. In fact, until that moment, he hadn't even thought about it. Something strange was happening, but what exactly was it?

The preacher walked back up to the center of the platform, faced the group, once again raising his hand toward heaven.

"Brothers and sisters, Christianity is not about what you can get out of God. It's a matter of what God can get out of you. Life is not about you—it's about what God wants to do through you. Believe me, the Lord will devise a far more dynamic future for your life with adventures more wonderful than you can ever concoct on your own. Nothing is too difficult for the Almighty, the Lion of Judah."

Cory had never heard a sermon like this before. What could God possibly get out of him? What did he have to offer God and why would God even want it? This man related to God as a person, not a theory, not a feeling, not some abstract concept or force drifting through the universe.

"Brothers and sisters, I am going to ask anyone who wants forgiveness of sins or help forgiving others to come forward. God wants you to have a fresh start. God loves you. He delights in those who repent and turn to him. When you come, remember, you are not coming up here for me. You are coming up to encounter God."

He gestured to the musicians who began playing an instrumental number.

"Paul, you might not believe this, but I just realized that for the past few days I have not craved one cigarette. At home, I smoked every day. Is it possible that God took that desire away, before I even asked him to?" asked Cory.

Paul, who had sat quietly throughout the sermon, gave him a warm, encouraging smile.

"Yes, it's possible and it sounds like he did."

He looked intently at Cory and then toward the pastor.

"Do you think you might like to go up there and thank God for what he did for you?"

As Cory watched dozens head up to the front by the platform, he turned to Paul and replied, "I don't know if I am ready to encounter God or not."

"I understand, but Cory, I hope you realize that God is very eager to encounter you. He always has been."

For some reason he could not explain, Cory, feeling motivated and confident, walked toward the preacher. He decided that if God wanted to meet him that badly, he should accept the invitation. As he approached the front of the tent, his remaining doubts seemed to drop off gradually one by one like dried autumn leaves swirling downward and then blowing away into the distance.

Up front, near the platform, Cory prayed some prayers of repentance with a counselor working with the pastor. It was as if a burdensome overcoat fell off of Cory's shoulders. He breathed easier and felt more at peace than he would have guessed possible.

After talking quietly to God for a few minutes, Cory returned to his seat and joined Paul. His host just sat there smiling. Cory felt grateful Paul did not ask questions about the experience. Those were moments to ponder and interpret over time. As the crowd dispersed, the two of them walked outdoors together into the evening air.

As promised, after the revival meeting, the adjacent tent was set up for a dance and an evening meal with the same band playing a variety of music. About a hundred, young people attended, mingling in small groups, enjoying dinner. Others ignored the food and focused on making friends and finding dance partners. Most of the adults ate and socialized in a separate tent.

"We'll be eating dinner here this evening. Feel free to mingle, and enjoy yourself. I wasn't planning on leaving for another hour or so. No rush," said Paul.

"That's fine. I'd like to eat dinner with you this evening."

The two of them walked toward the tent. Initially, the music was loud and fast-paced, but eventually changed to slow tunes.

As Cory and Paul entered the tent, they noticed the long table filled with food. Paul's crockpot filled with bratwurst and sauerkraut was already on the table along with numerous other entrees, side dishes, and desserts. Paul fetched two plates and served up a portion for himself and Cory. There was no possible way Cory would pass up Paul's cooking, not after devouring those delicious pancakes at breakfast. Sitting down at an empty table, the two of them began spreading Dijon mustard over the bratwurst and eating with gusto.

"How about a couple slices of cake and soda to wash it down?" asked Paul.

Cory nodded. "Yes, thank you."

As Cory observed the crowds of young adults socializing, he wondered which girl he should ask to dance. One gal was dressed in a rather expensive outfit: white jeans, a blue shirt, a white jacket, and a white matching cap. Her leather flats matched her outfit as well, perfect for dancing. She looked quite Chanel to say the least, like a model on the cover of a magazine. She sat watching the festivities. Later on, she joined one man to dance for a couple minutes and then sat down again.

Another gal in a beautiful, designer dress attempted to dance. She repeatedly stumbled over her own feet and almost knocked down her dance partner. As she moved rather clumsily about the tent, Cory thought it was like watching a comedy of errors, a series of silly moves worthy of an old Chaplin silent movie like he had seen in a high school film class. He turned his head and decided not to watch any more. He was afraid he would laugh and embarrass her.

Paul returned with two slices of German chocolate cake and the sodas.

Cory smiled. "This is the perfect ending to the meal."

"Glad you're enjoying it. After I finish eating, I'm going to talk with some friends. Feel free to hang out here."

After finishing the last bite of cake, Cory scanned the area and noticed another girl in torn jeans and a T-shirt on the other side of the tent. Actually, Cory could not have cared less if the girl had been wearing sackcloth and ashes. She was gorgeous with red hair and a captivating smile. She caught his attention and nodded at him. Opportunity stood there eyeing him, so there was no point in wasting valuable time. He walked over and introduced himself. She took his hand, went with him to the center of the tent, and slow danced.

Paul stood at the entrance of the tent for a moment pleased to see he had found a dance partner, and then left to chat with the minister and a few folks he recognized from town.

The girl looked into Cory's eyes and smiled.

"Hi, my name is Clarice Lyons."

"Good evening. I'm Cory Parker."

"Do you live around here?" she asked curiously, never taking her eyes off him.

Cory wished he could have answered in the affirmative.

"Sad to say that I don't. I am passing through, heading for Pittsburgh."

Much to his surprise, the girl looked ecstatic. Her eyes brightened and she gently squeezed his hand.

"I'm here with my folks this weekend for the revival and for a chance to get the last of my things out of the house. Next week, I'm moving into an apartment outside Pittsburgh. I lived there growing up, so I already know the area well," she said.

"Perhaps we will see each other again. I plan to move in with a friend in Pittsburgh. His house is just outside the city."

As Clarice danced with him, he got the feeling like they were the only two there. She was stunning.

"I see you got some dinner. Did you enjoy it?" Clarice asked.

"Yes, as a matter of fact. Have you eaten? Could I get you something?"

"Actually, I ate before I came tonight, since I'll be busy packing for the move, so I wasn't planning on staying very long, but I did prepare something for this evening."

"What did you make?"

"French Crepes topped with a sweet citrus mixture, mascarpone, strawberries, and whipped cream."

"Wow. That sounds exotic. Is there any left?"

Clarice glanced in the direction of the food table.

"No, all gone. They went fast."

"Sorry I missed out on that. Sounds like you are a gourmet."

"I wouldn't say that, but I do make certain things very well."

"You dance well too," said Cory, noticing her timing and gracefulness.

"I took some dance lessons for fun last summer."

"A beautiful girl who can dance and cook. How lucky for me."

At the other side of the tent, a young man sat staring at them, sipping a soda. After finishing the drink, he crumbled the paper cup into a ball and threw it on the ground. His eyes locked on Cory.

As casually as he could, Cory asked, "Clarice, do you know that guy sitting near the refreshment table?"

As they danced, Cory turned his partner around so she could take a quick glance at him. As she turned and faced Cory again, her expression changed. She looked dismal.

"That's an old ex-boyfriend, Cameron Dunkel. After all these years, he still wants me back. He can't take 'No' for an answer."

Clarice held Cory a little tighter.

"Let's go outside and talk," Clarice said quietly.

Glad to oblige, Cory walked with her into the fresh air. Immediately, Clarice seemed more relaxed.

"I'm sorry that happened. I really am having a good time. I just don't like having him around. He's been in my life far too long."

Cory noted a change in her voice.

"When did you two meet?"

"This will sound crazy, but it's the truth. Back in high school, one night, Cameron got drunk, wandered around the neighborhood, and passed out in our driveway. My dad found him the next morning when he went outside to get the newspaper. Good thing he didn't drive over him on his way to work. Any rate. Dad brought him inside for some coffee and breakfast. That's when we met. Cameron was two years older than I was, a senior, tall and handsome, and I was young and stupid. Cameron asked me out and despite the fact he obviously drank to excess, like an idiot, I agreed."

"Sounds like a rocky relationship from the start."

"That's an understatement. When I found out he was on the high school football team, I admired him. He was an award-winning athlete, but an awful boyfriend. He was too possessive of me. I found out later on that I was the only girlfriend he ever had. At first, I liked all the attention. Later on, he got too domineering. When he drank, it got even worse. He tried to control the relationship, you know, suffocate me by trying to be with me all the time, telling me what to do. I was drowning in a sea of phone calls. I got tired of the whole mess, so I broke up with him."

"That's understandable. No one wants freedom taken away."

Clarice nodded. "Cameron's problem is he only defines himself in terms of having a girlfriend or a wife. Without a girl, he views himself as nothing, inferior, a loser, which is ridiculous. Each person is more than just one thing, one label. We are all so much more than the trite categories where society likes to place us."

"Very profound and so true. Potential is limitless when you choose to move ahead unafraid. You can't waste your time fretting over what other people think about your life or career," said Cory, feeling more confident that leaving home was indeed the best course of action.

The last remaining rays of sunlight shone on Clarice's red hair, giving it a blazing sheen. Clarice glanced at the sunset and back at Cory.

"I'm sorry. I shouldn't unload my troubles on you. We should just enjoy the evening."

"No need to apologize. Say, Clarice, do you have a favorite place in the Pittsburgh area where you like to go for dinner?"

"Yes, I sometimes get together with college friends at a place called Sarafino's. It's a fantastic Italian restaurant on Crafton Avenue."

Clarice's ex had emerged in the entranceway of the tent and stood there, leering at them again. From Cameron's perspective, he had done nothing wrong. He was the one who had been betrayed, stabbed with rejection, ground to powder by an unappreciative, narcissistic wretch who had used him, leaving him to be swept away in a tide of isolation, drowning in abandonment. His self-deception was chronic. Cameron lived in a self-destructive world of disillusionment, where he was entitled to live in a constant state of pleasure, even at the expense of another's happiness. He thrived on the notoriety of his past and expected others to lavish him with praise and attention for bygone days of faded victory. Cameron's unjustified rage lay just under the surface of his counterfeit composure like a landmine ready to explode if anyone dared tread even ever so lightly on his nerves.

Sensing that their time to talk might be growing short, Cory whispered to Clarice, "I should be settled in Pittsburgh in a couple weeks. Let's meet at Sarafino's, just the two of us, on the last Saturday of the month at six o'clock for dinner. My treat. How does that sound?"

"Sounds wonderful. I'd like to see you again."

Cameron had taken a few steps closer to them and stopped, obviously interested in what they were saying.

Whispering, Cory said, "I am going to leave with my friend, Paul. I'll see you later on. Don't let that guy push you around. Be careful."

"See you in two weeks," she replied softly.

Cory gazed into her green eyes.

"Definitely."

Cory walked in the direction of Paul who was chatting with a few friends.

"I'm ready to go whenever you are. I plan to hit the road again tomorrow, so I really need to get to sleep."

As they drove back to the cabin, Paul commented, "Not that this really matters, but I noticed you danced with one of the girls who dressed down tonight, instead of with the ones in fancy outfits. Somehow, I found that refreshing."

"Well, Paul, I value genuine friendship with a sweet girl who wants to dance with me over wealth any day. You see, back in high school I discovered something. Casual gals always know how to be themselves. They're open and honest and exhibit their own special brand of class."

"I don't think I follow you."

"Well, Paul, let me put it this way. From my experience, money talks, but it can't waltz."

CHAPTER 4

The next morning, after a breakfast of Western-style omelets and steak fries, Cory phoned his friend Carl whom he had known since grade school. They had been best friends as kids, always inventing some new game or getting into mischief. In fact, Cory had even joined Carl's family on vacations to the beach on two occasions. Unlike other classmates over the years, Carl had kept in touch, even after he moved away from Chicago.

"Carl, it's Cory. How are you?"

"Doing fine. Good to hear from you. What's been happening?"

"I've been traveling and right now I'm heading your way," Cory replied.

"Any chance of getting together for a visit?"

"Well, Carl, actually, I'm calling because I need a place to stay. I'm job hunting right now. Can I stay with you at least until I find work? I want to get a job in Pittsburgh."

"Sure, Cory, you can move in with me and stay as long as you need. No problem. I have a new address: 790 Parkland Dr. in Pittsburgh. It will be great to see you again. The only thing is I will be out of town on a business trip for the next two days. You'll need to stay with someone else or in a motel till I get back."

"Can't you leave a door unlocked or put the key under the mat?"

"Sorry, Cory. Too risky. We have had some burglaries around here. Just one of the drawbacks of a big city like Pittsburgh. Besides, since I have only lived at this address for a month, I am not sure which neighbors I can trust with a key, but don't worry. Life will work itself out when you get here."

That was Carl, eternally optimistic.

"Thanks again, Carl. I'll see you in a few days. Take care." Cory hung up the phone with a sense of relief that his plans were unfolding as anticipated.

"Cory, I'll be glad to drive you to the bus station and pay for your ticket," Paul offered cordially.

Cory looked up, not too surprised, considering Paul's generosity in the past couple days.

"Paul, that would be fabulous. I have limited funds to survive on till I get a job and I have no idea how long that will take, so any help is really appreciated. Thanks."

Paul opened up a cupboard and handed Cory a package of dried fruit, a box of peanut butter crackers, and another box of a dozen protein bars.

"Here's a few nonperishables for your journey."

Along with the food, Paul handed him fifty dollars in small bills and a piece of paper with his name, address, and phone number.

"Keep in touch, Cory."

"I will. Thank you, Paul. You are incredibly kind. I am ready to go, whenever you are. Oh, I need to do one more thing."

Unzipping his backpack, Cory fished around for his packs of cigarettes, piled them up on the table, and then threw them in the garbage bag.

"I'll never want those again," said Cory triumphantly.

"You're right. You've been liberated. I'll meet you at the car," said Paul, beaming with delight.

Paul grabbed his car keys and headed for the driveway. As Cory climbed into the passenger's side of the Paul's pickup truck, Cory noticed a magnet on the metal dashboard that read "Lion of Judah" underneath an image of Jesus.

"Paul, last night I heard the preacher use that phrase," said Cory, pointing to the picture. "What does that mean?"

"The lion is the symbol of the Jewish tribe of Judah. Jesus's ancestors came from that tribe so he is associated with the lion. It also denotes his divinity and royalty."

"I never heard any of this before. Thank you for explaining it to me."

Within twenty minutes, they arrived at the bus station and Paul purchased the one-way ticket. Cory gave Paul a hug, thanked him again, and headed for the bus without looking back. He thought he might get emotional, if he did.

During the bus trip, Cory reflected on the events of the past several days. His encounters with Mr. Franklin and Mr. Jamison had enabled him to continue on his journey. It was as if some mastermind strategically positioned them there like an invisible chess player moving pieces that opened doorways while calculating outcomes for Cory's personal gain. Maybe the pastor was right. God really did care about him personally. At any rate, God understood his taste in women. Without a doubt, Clarice personified Cory's idea of beauty and sweetness. He silently thanked God for orchestrating his life and prayed for his safety on the next phase of the journey to Carl's house.

About two hours later, the bus arrived at the depot outside downtown Pittsburgh directly across the street from a motel. As he exited the bus, Cory walked over to the front office to register. The rates were cheap for the Pittsburgh area at only $120 a night, a special rate for that time of year. The motel was an older model from the 1950s, a motor lodge the kind where you park in front of your door, probably the last of its kind in the area. The office, a detached building, stood in the front. The motel itself rose two stories with an outside walkway on both levels. After signing in and picking up the key, Cory received a complimentary local newspaper from the desk clerk and headed up to his room on the second floor.

To get there, Cory had to walk through a corridor open on one side with a cement support structure on the other which held up a section of the second-floor walkway. Upon entering the room, he turned on a lamp by the desk, sat down with the newspaper, and began perusing the employment section. Many postings required applicants to have a college degree or prior experience in a particular field. After a half hour of scanning job openings, Cory came upon the following ad:

> Wanted: Person needed to feed and care for lion cubs at the Pittsburgh Zoo. Responsible for other job-related duties including clerical work and records keeping. A strong desire to work with animals is mandatory. Will provide necessary training. Minimum of a high school diploma is required. Applicant must be at least twenty-one years of age. Full-time position. Salary: $24 an hour. Benefits package. Paid vacation time. Paid overtime, if needed. Contact the zoo at the following number, if interested: (412) 665-3640. Ask for Daniel Franklin.

Cory stared at the ad in disbelief. Daniel Franklin, the truck driver's son. What were the odds of running across his name in the paper, let alone working with him not to mention a job working with animals? Perfect.

He wrote down the phone number and placed a call to the zoo. The head of human resources sounded delighted to speak with him. Cory introduced himself and within a few minutes had set up an interview with Mr. Franklin for the following day.

Around nine o'clock the next morning, Cory walked about a mile to the zoo complex. A receptionist greeted him and handed him some paperwork to fill out. For a current address, Cory wrote down Carl's location. About fifteen minutes later, a director entered the reception area and examined the completed form and a copy of his resume.

"Good morning, Mr. Parker. I'm Daniel Franklin. Thank you for coming."

Daniel was a tall, dark-haired gentleman, around thirty. He seemed quite amiable and interested in speaking with Cory.

"Hi, Mr. Franklin. I'm glad I got to meet you. Believe it or not, I met your father a couple days ago when I was traveling here from Chicago. Your dad gave me a lift. It's a small world, isn't it?"

Mr. Franklin looked at Cory somewhat amazed and smiled.

"Yes, it is. I'm glad you got to meet him. He's a wonderful man. Follow me, please."

Mr. Franklin walked into a large office, lined with book shelves and filing cabinets. A large framed poster of a lioness and two cubs hung on the back wall. A number of ferns, flowers, and potted palms arranged throughout the room on tables, pedestals and the window sill created the illusion of a small jungle. A window overlooked the entrance. Mr. Franklin sat down at the chair behind his desk.

"Well, Mr. Parker, tell me why you like the idea of working here."

"First of all, I love animals. To be honest, I don't want a job where I do nothing but sit behind a desk all day. This combination of responsibilities suits me fine. In high school, I won a national award for a research project on wild cats, focusing primarily on lions, so I know some things about them already, but I would love to learn more."

"That research paper sounds impressive. I would love to read that sometime. It sounds like you have a genuine love for animals."

"Definitely. I have a German shepherd back home that I raised from a pup. I wanted more animals, but my parents wouldn't allow it."

After interviewing Cory for about twenty minutes, Mr. Franklin asked, "Would you like to see the cubs now?"

"Yes, sir. I would."

The director escorted Cory to a large enclosed area where two lion cubs were sprawled out on a bed of straw, napping in the sun. The enclosure did not resemble a cage at all. It was about five hundred square feet and temperature controlled with two skylights. Two chairs and a large table stood at one end of the room.

"These are Justin and Jezebel, brother and sister. They are two months old. Justin tends to walk around the enclosure when I come in."

As if taking a cue from a stage director, Justin woke up, stretched, got to his feet, rather wabbly, and began to march around the perimeter of the enclosure.

"It's fascinating. Even at this young age, it is not too unusual to see male lions mark off their territory. That is exactly what he would be doing in the wild, if he were full grown, except, of course, over a larger expanse. Even as cubs, Justin would be ready, on a small scale, to fight for dominance in the pride with other cubs through playing and wrestling. It's instinct. Of course, at this age, while in this enclosure with his sister, his dominance can only be demonstrated in miniscule ways, hence the pacing," Mr. Franklin explained.

He paused to watch Justin as the cat took command of the enclosure. The cub's padded paws marched in steady syncopation to the beat of an unseen drummer, only pausing on occasion to realign themselves to reassure their proper balance. Motivated by primitive instincts, he silently claimed the area for himself as his wild heart beat with the survival instincts and courage of his ancestors. Each energized muscle desired to grow stronger as each step led him closer to his predestined role as a born leader of a pride, and the innate desire to protect and care for his future mate and offspring.

"If you have ever observed housecats, they do the same thing inside. They mark territory by pawing at the furniture and rugs. Outdoor cats mark off territory in their yard, as well as larger regions around the neighborhood. That is why you hear cats fight. They are expressing their disagreement over which one has territorial rights to a particular area. Subconsciously, I think all cat owners have a hidden desire to embrace lions."

"I'll bet from his perspective Justin thinks he is very brave," observed Cory.

"Yes, that's Justin. Seven pounds of raw courage," replied Daniel.

Eventually, Justin sat down and tried his best to roar, a brief, staccato sound, and not too loud, but indeed adorable. Meanwhile, Jezebel lay in the sun, licking her paws.

"Would you like to feed them?"

Cory smiled at the cubs and their cuteness.

"Yes, I would."

"Great. Come with me."

Walking across the zoo about fifty yards, Cory stopped to admire a stunning peacock who stood with his tail feathers fanned out. A moment later, the bird slowly rotated clockwise displaying its magnificent array of colors. Cory took out his phone and snapped a picture. Mr. Franklin waited for Cory to look at the bird more closely.

"Impressive, don't you think?"

"Yes, indeed. Beautiful. I guess this is how he earns his keep," commented Cory.

"Well, if he ever gets bored working here, he can always get a job at NBC."

Remembering the TV logo from reruns, Cory laughed. It would be refreshing to work for a boss with a sense of humor. Daniel's voice and mannerisms were tranquil. He wanted others to feel at ease. Indeed, he was a lot like his father.

After walking about another twenty yards, Mr. Franklin led him to a room with two deep sinks and various supplies. He pointed to a soap dispenser.

"Wash up to your elbows. When we're done, we are going to prepare the cubs' formula."

"I feel like a doctor prepping for surgery," said Cory as he lathered up his hands and arms.

"This is just a precautionary measure anytime we are working with food. It is a general sanitation rule for the zoo. Now, we fix the formula. It's the equivalent of baby formula for humans, except this is designed for cats."

"Mr. Franklin, how did the cubs get here? Were they born here or brought here from somewhere else?"

"Their mother was killed, so a refugee service in Africa sent them over here to keep them alive. They would die in the wild, of course, without their mother."

Mr. Franklin began mixing some powders with water, stirring vigorously. He explained to Cory the elements in each mixture, a combination of vitamins, protein, and calcium. Next, he poured half of the mixture into a baby bottle and had Cory do the same for the second bottle. Returning to the lions' enclosure, they sat down.

"Should we pick them up?" asked Cory.

"Yes. They know what the bottles signify. They'll come to us in a minute. With Justin, I recommend that you feed him while he sits straddled across your lap for balance or just let him sit on the floor. He can be feisty when he eats. He tends to pull on the bottle. He is stronger than he looks. After his feeding is over, you can hold him on your shoulder and stroke him. That will help him gain confidence in you and know that you are safe. This begins a bonding process. You and I are going to become their surrogate mothers, basically."

Mr. Franklin handed Cory a pair of thick, leather gloves as the cubs began to approach the two men. Cory put on the gloves with a look of curiosity on his face.

Mr. Franklin explained, "The gloves are to keep you from getting scratched. They may be just cubs, but their feet are already the size of a full-grown dog. If those cats scratch you, they can cause some serious damage. It's good to wear jeans when working with them like you are now."

As the cubs got closer, Cory noted the size of their paws. They were indeed almost the size of his German shepherds.

By now the lions had positioned themselves at their feet. Cory leaned over, stroked Justin on the head, raised him gently up onto his lap, and gave him the bottle. Once again, trying to exert his dominance, the cub grabbed onto the bottle with both paws, tugging at it fiercely, craving every drop.

"It's okay, Justin. I won't take it from you till you're done. You're a good boy. That's a good breakfast for you, isn't it? You like that?" asked Cory calmly.

In contrast, Jezebel sat still, one paw delicately embracing the side of the bottle with her back leaning up against Daniel. Cory noted how the female actually acted more "lady like." After about ten minutes, the milk was gone.

"Wow. I can't believe how strong Justin is for a baby. He grabbed that bottle like he hadn't eaten in days. For a moment, I thought he was going to snatch it right out of my hands. Now I know what it would have been like to feed Hercules as a baby. Someone should have named you Hercules, sweetheart."

Cory tried to reconcile how something so small and helpless could house such energy and power.

"At this age, they are fed every couple of hours. They have enormous appetites because they're growing so fast. By the time they are full grown, they will each weigh several hundred pounds. Justin will probably outweigh Jezebel by about a hundred pounds," Daniel explained.

After Justin finished the bottle, Cory carefully moved the cub to his shoulder, removed the gloves, and stroked his back. Mr. Franklin did the same with Jezebel. After about ten minutes of caressing, both cubs decided it was time for a nap. They squirmed to be let down and returned to their pile of straw in the sunshine and sprawled out, whereupon Jezebel began cleaning Justin's face, licking off droplets of formula, and then laid down beside him.

"She's very accommodating, isn't she?" said Cory laughing.

"Yes, she is. Maternal instinct kicking in perhaps."

Cory sat there watching the cubs sleep, sharing each other's body warmth and companionship just like two overgrown kittens.

"I noticed you were gentle with him, moved slowly, and spoke in low tones. That's exactly what you should do. Talking to him is part of the bonding process. He will learn to recognize your voice and associate you with nurturing. They will nap for about thirty minutes and then come back here to get some attention. Tonight, they will sleep soundly for about six or seven hours straight. That has been their general habit. We have them monitored with a closed-circuit camera. Cats are all quite different regarding behavior patterns and personalities. As they get older, I will teach you how to read their body language, so you understand when they are content or agitated. Just like people, sometimes they will want to be left alone."

"I'll bet they will be quite popular when the general public gets to see them."

"Indeed, they will be," said Mr. Franklin. "Right now, these two sure are popular with the staff, number one on the hit parade, so to speak. Everyone wants to see them."

The two sat there watching the cubs for almost thirty minutes and just as Mr. Franklin had predicted, the cubs got up, stretched a moment, and walked toward them. Cory carefully lifted Justin with both hands and placed the cub over his shoulder, massaging his head, neck, and back. Justin nuzzled the side of Cory's head and neck and then lay still, enjoying the attention.

Likewise, Mr. Franklin held Jezebel, rubbing her head and neck. She laid her head down on his shoulder in a state of bliss. After about ten minutes, the cubs both squirmed. Each caregiver turned the cub and began massaging their stomachs and shoulders, whereupon the cubs stretched out on their backs, fully engulfed in the pleasure of human contact.

"The massaging of a cub mimics the interaction of the lioness with her offspring. The cubs have already been accustomed to associating this kind of contact with affection and security. That is why they crave it. Of course, a massage is also good for the circulation, just like it is with humans. After they finish up a bottle, we always need to hold them and massage them gently, either right away or after their naps. This reinsures that the organs will function properly. Just like in a human, it isn't healthy to store up toxins. That is one of the benefits of the lioness licking the cubs. Massages also calm them, which helps with sleep and digestion. You did a good job hanging on to that bottle. Justin is quite strong for a two-month-old."

As Cory continued stroking the cub, Justin sat up, stretched, and snuggled against Cory's neck, making rumbling noises. Mr. Franklin watched the cub's affectionate interaction with Cory. The cat acted like the two of them were old friends, not new acquaintances.

"What do you feed them when they are bigger, Mr. Franklin?"

The director, still holding Jezebel, replied, "You can call me Daniel. When they are full grown, they will consume on average ten to eighteen pounds of meat a day, on a five-day feeding schedule. We feed them raw beef or horsemeat. They love it. For adult lions, we also have to check to make sure their water bowls are full. They drink a lot. By the way, may I call you Cory?"

"Sure. That's fine."

Daniel watched Cory hold Justin.

"So, Cory, are you still interested in this job position?"

"Yes, definitely. I would love to work with them."

Cory caressed Justin again and the cub let out a little roar.

"Wonderful. Well, the job is yours. You can start tomorrow. In the months ahead, when the cubs are bigger, I'll give you some additional training so you can go on working with them. Some cats bond with humans and accept them as a member of the pride for life."

Cory set the cub down on the floor.

"That sounds like job security. Thanks, Daniel."

"Come on back to my office. I'll fill you in on some more details. By the way, I ordered lunch for two, since I knew I would have an interview today. Hope you like Italian subs."

Cory, who had not eaten much since he had left Paul's cabin, felt delighted at the invitation. A cordial, hospitable boss was one more perk with the new job.

"That's great. I am famished."

The two of them sat down to two thick, foot-long subs, coleslaw, and a couple sodas. For Cory, this was another feast.

As Cory unwrapped his sandwich to enjoy his first substantial sustenance of the day, he said to Daniel, "I wanted to talk to you about something. Your Dad mentioned you had a vision of the Lord some years back after a car accident." Cory paused, noticing that Daniel had stopped eating. "I understand if you don't want to talk about something so personal, but I am curious as to what happened. Could you tell me what it was like to see the Lord?" asked Cory, brimming with curiosity.

Daniel set down his beverage and looked out the window at the blue October sky.

"It was beyond description. It's amazing to stand in front of someone who knows all your faults, and all the sins you have ever committed, but loves you regardless. It was a pleasant shock. He spoke in a gentle voice, but he was very firm. He told me to focus on the needs of others, not my own. He also said I should distinguish between what I wanted and what I truly needed. They are not the same. When he spoke, I felt the greed inside me disintegrate. I don't know how else to put it. Jesus said he wants me to pray each day that his will is done in my life. I guess it's all summed up in service, trust, and self-denial," explained Daniel.

Cory listened in awe. "I guess that helps you keep Jesus at the forefront of your life, in first place."

Daniel nodded. "Exactly. That's what I try to do. Pray, help the needy, and ask to be used to serve him and others as he sees fit. From that day on, I started to love people more and animals too," said Daniel, glancing over at the poster of the lions.

"Serving others? Like buying me lunch today? I appreciate that," said Cory.

Daniel nodded. "I'm glad you're enjoying it."

Cory paused and reflected on how one encounter with Daniel had given him several blessings simultaneously: a job, a believing friend, and the opportunity to see God's love in action.

"Thanks for sharing that message with me, Daniel. Not everyone would open up like that," said Cory, sincerely grateful to obtain one more ray of wisdom.

"My pleasure. I'm glad you're seeking the Lord. He is worth knowing on so many levels," said Daniel, as he finished his sandwich. "Well, Cory. I will see you tomorrow morning around nine. Glad everything is working out."

Overjoyed with his immediate success at finding work, Cory headed back for the motel. He couldn't wait to tell Carl he had found a job. The sensation of victory acquired from his first attempt at a job search left him exhilarated.

Upon arriving at the breezeway that led to the motel rooms, Cory noticed a man off to his left in the parking lot, about twenty yards away, leaning up against a blue sports car, eyeing him. Aside from Carl, Clarice, and his aunt, Cory knew no one in the Pittsburgh area. The man stood in the shadow of the building, so Cory could not see his face too clearly; nevertheless, Cory sensed he was being watched.

As Cory walked along, the man stood up and began moving across the parking lot, heading for the end of the corridor. Instinctively, Cory picked up his pace slightly and the man did likewise, matching his steps, stride for stride, aiming for the opposite end of the breezeway, the direction where Cory was walking. If they both kept moving in their chosen routes, they would intersect at the end of the breezeway. Suddenly, Cory remembered what Carl had told him about crime in the area. What did this man have in mind? Robbery, assault, kidnapping?

In front of Cory stood the cement wall which supported the upstairs walkway. As Cory approached the wall, he kept saying to himself, "Think fast. There has to be a way out of this." He knew if he kept walking straight ahead he would collide with the stranger. Even though Cory was trained to defend himself, he saw no point in unnecessary risk. After all, the man could be armed. Unsure of the man's intent, Cory recognized the need to come up with an immediate plan of action, nonconfrontational and swift. He had learned years ago it was always far better to outthink scoundrels than to play the game their way.

At that moment, Cory devised a plan. He stopped just to the other side of the cement wall, hoping the pursuer had not changed course. Several vending machines blocked the view of the man who would be coming the other way. Cory quickly glanced around the wall in time to see the man walk behind the other end of the cement structure. Fortunately, he had not noticed Cory looking at him. Within seconds, Cory could hear the man approach, moving down the breezeway just the other side of the vending machines.

With seconds to spare, Cory initiated his scheme. He cut diagonally across the parking lot about fifteen yards, unseen, heading for the stairs that led to the second floor and his room. The cement wall served as a barrier, concealing his change of direction. Luckily, he had worn his tennis shoes which allowed him to move quickly with stealth.

Hurrying up the stairs, Cory glanced back at the same instant the man emerged from the other side of the cement wall, in front of the back doors that led to the motel office. Expecting to find Cory, the man stopped and stood there looking from side to side, puzzled, before glancing through the glass doors. From this angle, Cory was still unable to see his face, only the back of his blond head.

Since the man faced away from him, Cory easily proceeded up the stairs undetected and headed straight along the outside corridor for his room. Cory watched as the man reversed direction, realizing that somehow his target had evaded him. Appearing on the other end of the breezeway, just beyond the wall, the man stopped again almost directly below where Cory was moving noiselessly along the upstairs walkway.

Over and over again, Cory prayed silently, "Don't let him look up. Don't let him look up."

He didn't. Instead, the man continued straight ahead to the back side of the building and out of sight.

Cory sighed. By this time, he had arrived at his room. Opening the door, he double checked the lock in the doorknob, stepped into the room, closed the door quietly, secured the chain and deadbolt, and closed the blinds. He stood there a moment, relieved to feel safe inside. Whoever the predator was, he did not know where Cory had gone. For now, that's all that mattered.

After all, the motel had over two hundred rooms. At this point, without an exhaustive door to door search, it would be impossible for that man to figure out where Cory was staying. Besides, knocking on everyone's door would be too conspicuous. To be safe, he decided if anyone knocked, he would not open the door. After all, if for some reason members of the managerial staff wanted to speak with him, they could always phone.

After composing himself, Cory called the front desk to report a suspicious character in the breezeway and was told the police would be notified. The motel manager expressed no interest in tangling with a stranger and no one else was available to deal with the situation.

Out of curiosity, Cory went to the window, separated the blinds slightly, and peered out. His suspicions were correct. The stalker had returned to the parking lot and was still looking for him, pacing around, stopping, and turning to look in different directions. He seemed totally mystified, clueless, unsure of how to proceed.

As Cory watched, he had to laugh. From that man's perspective, it must have seemed as if Cory had disappeared into thin air like a phantom. Perhaps the man felt like he was chasing a mirage or some hallucination. Cory stood there smiling. He had outwitted the pursuer at his own game by employing two of his skills: physical speed and speed of mind.

Consequently, instead of being the victim, Cory was now the one conducting his own version of reconnaissance, spying on the enemy, unnoticed, from a motel window. With the blinds already closed, Cory pulled the drapes shut and turned on a light, leaving the perpetrator to roam aimlessly to no avail in the parking lot below.

Sitting on the edge of the bed, kicking off his shoes, Cory decided he would stay in for the rest of the evening. After all, he had already enjoyed a substantial lunch courtesy of Daniel Franklin, plus he had food in his backpack courtesy of Mr. Jamison. He also still had the two granola bars he got from the truck driver, Daniel's father, as well as a few candy bars.

Upon further reflection, Cory decided he would call the front desk and ask for assistance with his belongings in the morning. That way if he did encounter anyone in the process of checking out, he would not be alone. In addition, he would take a cab to Carl's house; that would be safer than walking three miles under the circumstances.

Still, Cory kept wondering who the man was and why he tried to confront him.

CHAPTER 5

The next morning, as planned, Cory got assistance with his backpack and sleeping bag from the motel's assistant manager. Exiting the motel room, Cory examined the parking lot carefully to see if anyone else was outside. Aside from a half dozen cars, the area was deserted. No motel guests. No stalker. Cory noticed that the sports car was gone.

As Cory and the bellman walked up to the front desk to check out, the manager gave Cory a concerned look. "I trust you slept well after your incident, Mr. Parker. I wanted to reassure you that I do have a security system in place." The manager seemed rather worried about the reputation of his business establishment. "When guests arrive with an automobile, their cars are registered with us for the duration of their stay." The manager held up a large index card. "We record the license plate number as well as the color, make, and model of the vehicle. Every evening I do a security check of the parking lot. Yesterday, I checked the cards and one car did not match up: a blue Stingray. It's hard not to notice a car like that. I reported that to the police along with your report of being followed. The police arrived ten minutes after I called them, but the officers found no one in the parking lot that matched your description. The Stingray was also gone. Whoever that was, he was not registered at this motel. I just wanted you to know."

"Thank you, sir. I appreciate your efforts. Here's the key," said Cory, placing the motel key on the counter. He felt relieved to get out of that motel unscathed and grateful for the opportunity to get settled at his new residence. After hailing a cab, Cory took off for Carl's house, feeling a sense of safety. If the predator were still in the area somewhere, he would have no idea in which direction Cory had headed.

Upon arriving at his new location, Cory tipped the cab driver, and headed up the front steps. Before Cory had a chance to knock, he heard a dog bark, and Carl opened the door, arms outstretched. He had not changed since the last time they had met. His black hair was still cut short and his brown eyes beamed with joy.

"Hey, Cory! Welcome to your new home. It's so good to see you again," said Carl, giving him a hug.

Cory stepped inside to a spacious living room with a brick fireplace. A silky haired Golden Retriever ran up to him, tail wagging, begging for attention.

"This is Samson, my buddy."

"What a beautiful dog. I have a German shepherd back home. Someday I want him to live with me again."

Leaning his head against Cory's knee, Samson sat contented as Cory stroked his head.

"He can tell you like him. That's why he took to you right away. He barks, if someone shows up at the door, unless I open it first. He's generally protective of me," said Carl, rubbing Samson's head and shoulders.

"Thanks for letting me stay here, Carl. I don't know what I would have done without you."

"Follow me and I will show you where you're staying."

Carl led Cory downstairs to the basement, fully furnished, with its own separate bedroom and bath. Samson followed them, excited to have a visitor. The dog always assumed everyone who showed up at the front door was there to see him.

"The downstairs is all yours."

"Wow, Carl, this is wonderful. It's like my own apartment."

Carl pointed to a side door. "You can even use your own private entrance. Just be careful to always keep it locked. Here's your keys, one for the front door and one for your side entrance."

Cory set his belongings on the bedroom floor. The room was simple, but adequate. It included a double bed, nightstand, dresser, a chair, and two lamps, plus a large light fixture in the ceiling. The adjacent living room contained a large sofa with a matching chair, two end tables with brass lamps, a wool rug, a widescreen TV, and a large brick fireplace. Since it reminded him so much of Paul's cabin, Cory instantly felt at home.

"How about breakfast? I don't have to leave for work until nine o'clock."

Cory felt gratitude welling up inside him.

"Yes, that's perfect."

The two of them headed upstairs and began preparing eggs, bacon, and toast. Cory offered to fix a couple of omelets with cheese and onion. As he scrambled up the eggs, he looked at Carl.

"I have to tell you about my new job at the zoo. You aren't going to believe this, but I'm working with lions."

Carl stopped turning the bacon, stared at Cory, and grinned.

"Really? No kidding? I hope your life insurance policy is paid up and your will is up to date. If there is anyone you want to say 'goodbye' to, I would do it now."

Cory laughed. "It's not like that. These are just cubs. I'm responsible for feeding them, cleaning up after them, and handling some of their paperwork. I was at the zoo yesterday feeding them. I really enjoyed it. They are so sweet."

"I am glad to hear they're babies. I was having visions of you needing a whip and a chair to control them like the ringmaster at Barnum and Bailey's. Well, as long as you like the work, that is what matters most."

The two sat down to eat, plates loaded with food. The bacon reminded Cory of the breakfast he shared with Paul a few days ago.

"So, Carl, what's your job like?"

"I am the head of an advertising agency. I coordinate ad campaigns and generate slogans and images mostly for new products, anything at all: soda, soap, wine, cars, appliances, clothes, candy. The company also handles ads for services like travel agencies, auto repair, and grocery chains. It's a creative job."

"You double-majored in marketing and business management, didn't you? I remember you wrote me about your classes."

Cory pondered a moment about Carl's brilliance in awe of his accomplishments. Carl thrived on perseverance which resulted in enormous strides of success both in high school and in the business world. He either walked around life's obstacles or plowed through them at top speed. He remained confident in his creative abilities but was smart enough to acknowledge his limitations. As a result, he had developed a network of experts in various fields, primarily photography and computer graphics, individuals who could pick up the slack in areas where Carl lacked proficiency. The end result was always the same; he got the job done.

"Say, Carl, maybe the zoo would like some ads for their new cubs? They will draw a great deal of attention when the public can finally see them. I could mention it to my boss, Mr. Franklin, if you like."

Carl nodded. "Sure, why not? It can never hurt to ask. Go ahead and mention my name and give him this."

Carl took his wallet out and handed Cory one of his business cards.

"He can give me a ring, if he is interested. I'm sure I can come up with several good ideas for him. He can choose the approach he likes best."

After breakfast, Carl dropped off Cory at the zoo and then headed downtown to his office, a large corner room with floor to ceiling windows overlooking one section of the Pittsburgh skyline and a wide stretch of the Allegheny river. After entering the room, and logging into his computer, he began opening the morning mail.

A few minutes later, he heard a knock and there in the doorway stood a new member of his advertising team. He had just arrived in Pittsburgh and this was his first day on the job.

"Good morning, Mr. Christianson. I wanted you to know that I have been discussing the Stevenson account with James and we are in the process of coming up with a slogan for the dog food commercial."

Carl looked up from his business letter.

"Good morning. I'm sure you and James will come up with something. I'll meet with the two of you later in the week to see what options you have for your presentation."

Although Carl was quite laid back in his private life, at the office, he was all business. Efficiency, creativity, and teamwork constituted the building blocks of the advertising infrastructure and everyone on Carl's floor knew it. Last year, Carl had helped net the company over twenty million dollars in advertising sales and he had received accolades from top ranking business associates and customers alike.

"So tell me. Have you gotten settled in your apartment yet?" Carl asked.

"No, I will be in the apartment this evening. Last night I had to stay in a motel. The moving van is arriving right after work."

"Sounds like you have everything planned out. Well, I need to get back to the mail, so I will plan on speaking with you and James later in the week."

Carl studied the large desktop calendar.

"Let's say Thursday at eleven o'clock. That's about the only free time I will have to interact with you guys and discuss photo and slogan options."

He wrote down the time with their names on his desktop calendar.

"Fine. I'll tell James."

The new employee left the office and headed back down the hall to his work cubical. Carl continued reading emails and prioritizing his obligations for the day. On the top of the list, he needed to finish the budget proposal for the latest advertising campaign. Afterward, he contacted several photographers to schedule them for a photo shoot for a travel agency. The next step was to address a new batch of emails and write up a job description for one more finance officer, a necessary hire to take on additional work in an expanding corporation.

About two hours later, the phone rang.

"Carl, this is Cory. Mr. Franklin likes the idea of advertising the cubs in the local paper. He would like you to take some photos of them and write some catchy phrase to gain the readers' attention. In addition, he would like you to contact some local radio stations to spread the word. I'll give you one of his business cards with his contact information when I see you tonight."

Leaning back in his office chair, Carl looked out over the skyscrapers of the city. His windows offered a spectacular view of the cityscape, the river, and boats cruising along.

"Wonderful. Tell him I'm interested in the project and that I work with some excellent freelance photographers. I will schedule one of them to come over there when it's convenient for him. I need to go, but I'll talk to you tonight. Bye."

As Cory hung up the phone, Daniel walked into his office.

"Good news. Carl says he is interested in taking on the advertising campaign for the cubs. He will send a photographer over whenever it fits your schedule."

Daniel looked delighted.

"I'll get back to him about the date, but I think sometime in the afternoon would be best around two o'clock. I have a lot of meetings for the next several days with the budget department, security team, and veterinarians and I have to order more supplies. Later on, my schedule will open up. If the photographer comes in the afternoon, the cubs will be having lunch. Hopefully, they will be active so the photographer can get some good shots."

Cory nodded. "I'll tell him tonight at dinner."

"Dinner? Do you two know each other that well?"

"Yes. Actually, we share a house. He is my best friend."

Daniel smiled. "Well, it sounds like a splendid arrangement for you. I need to make some phone calls, so I'll see you."

Cory sat in his office reflecting on the day's accomplishments. Life was turning out for the best. He was settled into a new job and a welcoming home. Now he could actually pay Carl rent instead of relying on charity. His sense of independence manifested itself more and more each day.

Cory thought to himself, *You can't call me a kid anymore, Dad. You can't say I won't amount to anything. I just wish you could see all this for yourself.*"

CHAPTER 6

*T*wo weeks later, Cory looked forward to his scheduled rendezvous with Clarice at the Italian restaurant: Sarafino's. Hopefully, nothing would prevent her from getting there. Cory would have willingly hiked the entire length of the Appalachian Trail, if Clarice were waiting for him at the end. He had reminisced about her for days, looking forward to knowing her better. Somehow, those green eyes were still watching him.

By late afternoon, Cory had located the address and phone number of the restaurant. Since he had cashed his first paycheck, he had enough to treat himself and Clarice to dinner and extra for cab fare. The other cash that he had brought from home, along with the fifty dollars from Mr. Jamison, was safely deposited in a local bank. Now that he held a job, that money would be reserved as an emergency fund, another necessary part of his independence.

As he got ready for the date, he thought about asking Carl to drop him off but decided against it. He didn't want Carl to have a chance of meeting Clarice until sometime later on. After all, Carl was single, tall, rich, and charming. Friend or no friend, why invite competition?

As the cab pulled up in front of the restaurant, Cory felt the anticipation of a great meal with a fantastic redhead. He walked in and found her already seated at a table for two, looking as lovely as the evening they met. She smiled and waved. The situation felt surreal, but there she was, together with him once again. She stood up, embraced him, and kissed him gently on the cheek. Cory stared a moment into her green eyes and returned the kiss.

"I am so glad you remembered. I was a little afraid you had forgotten or something would stand in the way of your getting here," Clarice said softly.

Cory felt mesmerized. It was like discovering treasure in his back yard and coming to the joyful realization that all the diamonds were his.

"Thanks for accepting the invitation. This place looks pretty popular. I'm glad you recommended it."

As the two of them sat down, a waiter walked by with a plate of veal parmigiana with spaghetti smothered with meat sauce and placed it front of another customer at an adjacent table. Another waiter quickly set the table next to them with flatware rolled up in linen napkins and a glass vase of fresh flowers. The smell of garlic, basil, oregano and other aromas drifted into the room from the kitchen.

Clarice stared at Cory's chestnut brown hair and deep-set, brown eyes. She handed Cory a dinner menu and began bubbling over in nervous excitement.

"I love eating here. One of the specialties is 'greens and beans' with sausage. It's made with spinach, white beans, and a splash of white wine for flavor. It's quite good, but they have other basic Italian dishes as well. One unusual item is wild boar meatballs."

Cory's eyes widened. "Seriously? That's different. I should order that just so I can tell my friends I ate it."

He tried to peruse the menu but found himself staring at Clarice. Eating dinner with her felt dreamlike. They were actually alone, and best of all, that ex-boyfriend was nowhere in sight to spoil the evening. They had managed to create their own miniature vacation to Italy without the hassle of passports, airline tickets, and unwelcomed guests like Cameron.

After placing their orders, Clarice focused her full attention on Cory. He acted differently from other men she had met. He had gentler mannerisms and a soft-spoken voice that made her feel relaxed. Everything about him communicated one simple message: You can trust me.

"So, Clarice, what have you been doing, since I last saw you?"

"Well, I moved the last of the boxes into my friend's apartment. I'm all set up now. The apartment has a large kitchen, which I make use of every day. You know I like to cook." She paused. "One reason I moved to Pittsburgh was to put some distance between me and Cameron. Unfortunately, a girlfriend told him where I was headed and a few more details. I had a long chat with her about keeping quiet where I am concerned; otherwise, she and I can't be friends anymore."

She looked up at the ceiling. Cory sensed that talking about Cameron had left her feeling rather rattled, but she continued.

"A week ago, I finished my final exam for my last online college course in journalism, and I lined up a full-time job with a newspaper right here in Pittsburgh. What about you?"

As the waiter set down two glasses of Italian soda, and two orders of 'greens and beans' along with some freshly baked Italian bread, Cory summarized how he came down by bus, spent a few nights in a motel, and then moved into his friend's house. He did not mention the incident with the stalker. After all, what would be the point in worrying her?

Looking down at the plate of food, Cory commented, "This looks wonderful. Thanks for suggesting it."

"I'll bet you like it," Clarice said confidently.

"Would you mind if I said grace?" asked Cory.

"Please, go right ahead."

"Lord, thank you for this special time with Clarice. Thank you for this meal. Please bless this food and bless us, your children. Amen."

"Thanks, Cory. That sounded like it came straight from your heart."

She glanced about the restaurant.

"The waiters here are extremely friendly and attentive. Everyone gets served quickly. It's as if the waiters all know the customers personally. Those are some of the main reasons I keep coming back, that and the food, of course. This place has a lot of regulars, especially on weekends," Clarice stated.

As she spoke, a waiter walked by with a tray of lasagna and salad.

"You might recall I mentioned my folks live near Titusville. Do your folks originate from Pennsylvania or elsewhere?" asked Clarice curiously.

"Both of my parents are from Hazelton. My father attended Penn State. When I was in high school, we drove all the way from Chicago to watch Penn State play Navy at Beaver Stadium. Penn State won twenty-one to seven. Dad was so happy he sang the Penn State fight song most of the way home. Roar, lions, roar! He drove my mother half crazy. To this day, my father would rather watch a Penn State game than eat, if that is the choice. He loves the Nittany Lions."

They ate for a few minutes in silence. Cory made note of Clarice's lovely pink dress and the way she had fixed her hair differently. Instead of letting it fall straight down, she had brushed the sides back and held them together with a fancy hair clip, the same color as her dress. The hairstyle showed off her facial features very becomingly.

"Clarice, you are never going to guess what kind of work I'm doing now. I'm working with lions at the zoo."

Initially, Clarice's expression looked identical with Carl's when he had found out. She stared at him.

"You must be a brave man. Have you worked with wild animals before?"

"They're only cubs, Clarice. Sweet, loving babies. I feed them their formula every few hours that I am at work and massage them. In between times, when they are sleeping, I handle some paperwork, respond to emails, and answer the phone, but working with the cubs is the best part. It might sound strange, but I feel like a parent."

Cory took out his wallet and handed Clarice a business card.

"Here you go. Just in case you have a chance to come by sometime. By the way, my new home phone and cell number are on the back. Would you mind giving me your number? I would really like to call you sometime, so we can go out again."

Clarice listened graciously, taking in every word. She glanced at both sides of the card, tucked it into her wallet, then reached into her purse, tore off a piece of paper from a small notebook, and jotted down two numbers.

"There you go. That's the new number at the apartment and the bottom one is my cell. I don't have any business cards yet."

She paused, pondering his new job situation. Cory was unique in so many ways.

"I'm so glad you found something you really enjoy. I hope it's rewarding for you. If I come by the zoo, could you show me around?"

"Absolutely. I can probably get special permission for you to see the lion cubs. I think you would enjoy that. We can have lunch together too. Let me know when you can come so I can make arrangements."

At that moment, the waiter arrived with two plates of fettuccine with wild boar meatballs on the side and slices of garlic bread. The presentation was exquisite.

"Thank you. We are going to enjoy this," said Cory.

"You are welcome, sir. Will there be anything else at the moment?"

Clarice looked up at Cory. "I'm fine."

Cory smiled. "I guess for right now we are all set. We might get something else later on."

Cory wasn't sure whether to begin eating or first snap a picture of the entrée, then he got a better idea.

"Hey, Clarice. Before we start eating, let's take a selfie."

Cory got down on one knee beside Clarice and put his arm around her shoulders.

The waiter, noticing their efforts to get a good shot, walked over and said, "Please, allow me. I'll get a good closeup. There. How is that?"

The two of them examined the photo. He had lined up a perfect picture of the two of them.

"Looks great. This will make a wonderful memento of the evening. Thanks," said Cory.

The waiter smiled, cleared a table of its dirty dishes, and headed back for the kitchen.

"I guess he earned his tip for this evening," said Cory almost laughing as he returned to his chair.

Eager to try this new culinary experience, he began cutting into the meatballs and trying a bite.

"This is an unusual flavor. I am not quite sure how to describe this. The fettucine is excellent too. What do you think? Do you like it?"

Instead of responding, Clarice stared out the front window. She gasped, holding her breath. She did not seem to notice when the fork slid out of her hand, landing on the plate. The warm glow in her cheeks disappeared. Her body became rigid, catatonic, like a snared animal paralyzed in a state of shock.

"Clarice, what's the matter?"

Cory turned to see a tall, blond man glaring at them. He stood on the sidewalk like an iron statue, motionless, lifeless, with a cold deadly stare in his eyes. A minute later, he walked away and drove off in a blue sports car at high speed. Clarice looked at Cory.

"He followed me here. He knows I love this restaurant. Why can't he just leave me alone. Dumb jerk."

Slowly, Cory asked, "Clarice, was that your old boyfriend?"

Having only seen Cameron once before a few weeks ago, Cory reflected a moment, and felt convinced that this was the same man who had tried to confront him in the motel parking lot. That was definitely the same blue sports car. Reliving that moment of alarm, he chose to put that thought out of his mind. He would deal with Cameron later, if necessary. For now, he was determined to focus on Clarice. She had become a priority in his life. For a moment, Cory thought Clarice was going to cry, but she composed herself, sipped her drink, and sighed.

"Yes, it was. That was Cameron."

"Don't worry. He's gone now, so let's just enjoy this meal. I have never tasted anything like this before." Cory paused. "We'll do something different next time. We'll go somewhere else, someplace he won't show up."

Clarice began eating her dinner, slowly and methodically, as if she had to concentrate on each step of an intricate process.

"Clarice, tell me some more about your job. You mentioned journalism and working for a newspaper. Are you a writer or an editor? Do you hold interviews?"

Acting more relaxed, Clarice enjoyed a bite of food and leaned back in the chair.

"I write for the *Pittsburgh Post-Gazette*. Of course, I edit my own work, but on occasion I put in overtime and edit other articles as well. I've been enjoying it so far. It's challenging and you get to meet some interesting people."

"What people? Anyone famous?"

"Well, so far I have interviewed the mayor about some zoning issues and the quarterback for the Pittsburgh Steelers. Everyone who loves football around here is a Steelers fan, including me. Of course, we are all praying for another Super Bowl victory. The Eagles won last year, but at least that is another Pennsylvania team."

Clarice began eating her meal more enthusiastically. The atmosphere of oppression and dread seemed to have lifted almost as quickly as it came. She smiled and enjoyed another bite of fettucine. "This is really quite good. I'll have to order this again sometime."

"I have seen a couple of Steelers games thanks to my aunt who lives in the area. My parents, my aunt, and I got tickets to several football games over the years when I was growing up. We would come here from Chicago to visit her. I don't know how, but she could always manage to get the best tickets. Great seats. I think she knows someone who works for the team. I love the sport, but right now I would have to save my money before I could afford tickets."

"What else do you like besides football?"

"Well, I usually don't tell people this, but I was the Chicago Golden Gloves Champion a couple years ago. I was a member of a fight club and competed for a few titles. I loved getting into the ring and workouts helped me keep in shape. I was a smoker as a kid, but when I took up boxing, I quit for a while. Smoking slowed me down. I couldn't get enough air. At this point, I don't think I'll smoke again. Ever since I left home and headed for Pittsburgh, I have not had one craving for a cigarette. It's a bad habit. Who needs it?"

Clarice looked impressed. "Wow. A real fighter. I never knew anyone like that before. I'm glad you gave up the cigarettes. I hate the smell of smoke."

As discreetly as possible, she checked out his biceps and shoulders. He looked like a man who could bench press a couple hundred pounds and handle himself in a boxing match. More importantly, she admired him for being sincere and considerate.

"I also like swimming," Cory continued. I participated on the swim team in high school. I'm a good swimmer, but I never won any awards. I wasn't fast enough. I just enjoyed it, especially all the comradery with the guys. I loved going off the high dive. Some people are afraid of heights, but not me. My endurance is okay, I suppose. I can swim about a half mile or so and then I need a break. The other thing I enjoy is boating. I like all kinds of boats. Sailboats, rowboats, kayaks, paddle boats, cruise ships. I remember my dad taking me for a boat ride on the Alleghany River, when I was about seven."

"Maybe we could do that sometime. I enjoy boat rides too," Clarice responded fervently.

"I was thinking the same thing," said Cory, feeling elated. He had never felt so relaxed around a woman before.

Clarice reached across the table and put her left hand on top of Cory's.

"I would like to spend some more time with you."

This was the same look and the identical soft tone Clarice expressed when they danced the night they met. Cory now understood the same rush of nostalgia like his grandfather must have felt when he described parking his 1957 Chevy at a drive-in the night he kissed a girl for the first time.

"I'll think of some places where we can go and call you later on."

"I'm looking forward to that, Cory."

The two of them finished dinner and contemplated which dessert would best round off the meal.

"And how is everything at this table?"

"Well, we are thinking about dessert. Would you recommend the Italian cake or...?"

Cory looked up from the menu at Clarice who at the same moment gasped. Her eyes stared, transfixed. Cameron stood beside their table, leering at her. Cory quickly stood up and took a step backward.

"Cameron, leave us alone! Go, now," Clarice said boldly, attempting to mask her fear behind the volume and sharp tone of her voice.

Cameron glared at Cory and turned his stare again toward Clarice.

"Who is this guy? What are you doing with him? Why is he here?"

Clarice held her ground.

"This is none of your business, Cameron. Stop interfering in my life and leave me alone. Get out!"

Other customers in the restaurant began looking in their direction, exchanging comments. Some of the patrons sitting closer to them pushed their chairs back. A few headed for the door, anticipating a fight.

Cameron, with his eyes still locked on Clarice, grabbed her by the arm and yanked her to her feet.

"You are my girl. You are coming with me, if you know what's good for you. You got that?" he bellowed.

Clarice made a futile attempt to wrench herself free from his tight grip. In an instant, Cory latched onto Cameron's arm, squeezing it like a tourniquet.

"You let her go, now!" yelled Cory, like a police officer firing a warning shot into the air.

Immediately, Cameron released his grip on Clarice, turned, twisted his arm free from Cory's grasp, and swung at his face. Cory ducked and punched Cameron in the diaphragm and planted an uppercut, snapping his head backward. He fell and hit the floor barely missing another table. The couple sitting there grabbed their precious plates of linguini and clams and ran to the front of the restaurant to avoid a collision. Cameron lay there a moment, dazed, and staggered to his feet. Eyes blazing, he swung his fist at Cory who tried to block the punch but got struck in the jaw. He fell back against the wall and recovered in time to dodge a second blow. Cameron's fist hit the wall missing the window and Cory's jaw by an inch.

Meanwhile, Clarice ran back into the kitchen to get help from the manager and staff. In the midst of the brawl, Clarice pointed out the assailant to the cook who emerged still holding his frying pan. At that moment, Cory had just been shoved backwards toward the kitchen door. Upon seeing the frying pan, Cory grabbed it from the cook, grasped the skillet firmly with both hands and slammed it full force into Cameron's forehead, knocking him out cold. If Cameron's head had been a baseball, Cory could have knocked it out of the park.

Several customers stood up and applauded shouting, "He got just what he deserved."

Some customers returned to their seats to finish their meals. Other restaurant patrons remained standing outside, plates and forks in hand, still eating their dinner, having watched the events unfold through the windows unconvinced that it was safe to reenter the dining area.

Cory leaned against the wall, in no mood to take a bow. He was simply relieved that the confrontation had come to an abrupt halt. While the manager phoned the police and emergency dispatch, Clarice walked with Cory back to the kitchen to put ice on his jaw.

"Thank you for defending me and standing up to him. Cameron is such an animal. I swear. If jealousy and brutality were Olympic events, he would win the gold medal."

Placing ice in a towel, Clarice handed it to Cory who pressed it carefully against his jaw.

"One summer Cameron was in New York City with some of his drinking buddies, hanging out at the YMCA, going to bars, and walking around Central Park. Well, he got into an argument with a cop and it almost turned into a fist fight. Cameron's friend held him back and moved him away from the officer," said Clarice.

Cory looked shocked. "He tried to pick a fight with a New York City cop? Who in his right mind would try that? Those officers tangle with terrorists, street gangs, and drug lords for heaven's sake. What makes Cameron think they would back down for the likes of him? That's nuts."

"You got that right."

Cory moved the ice a little lower along his jaw. The pain was gradually decreasing and the swelling was starting to go down.

"I've knocked opponents out before but never with a frying pan. That was a first. My trainer would have been proud of me for being innovative, but I should have moved faster. Next time, I won't underestimate him."

"Hopefully, there won't be a next time."

Two police officers entered the kitchen and asked them to come out and identify the culprit. After gathering details from eyewitnesses, the police carried Cameron to an ambulance, arresting him on charges of assault and battery. The customers and staff all agreed this was a case of self-defense. The other man clearly acted as the aggressor, and Cory had no choice but to render the assailant unconscious.

"He shouldn't be bothering us for some time," Cory said, smiling at Clarice with confidence.

Clarice stood looking out the window as the ambulance drove off.

"I don't know, Cory. Cameron has this uncanny habit of showing up where you least expect him."

CHAPTER 7

The trees in Carl's yard swayed with the evening breeze framed against dense cloud cover. A quick cloudburst fell for about ten minutes which converted into a light mist, barely noticeable. The house, normally picked up and ready for company, was in disarray. The dishes in the kitchen sink remained stacked about a foot high, waiting to be cleaned and returned to their assigned space in the cupboard. Carl's face looked as dismal as the weather.

In an attempt to brighten up Carl's mood and to thank him for his hospitality, Cory had fixed a baked ham, macaroni and cheese, and a garden salad, which were Carl's favorites. Regardless, for some reason, Carl did not display his jovial, positive self. Instead, he seemed rather introverted and unresponsive, atypical behavior for Carl.

"Carl, did you have a tough day at work?"

"You could say that. I am trying to figure something out," said Carl without looking up from his dinner plate.

Carl looked pensive as he sipped his coffee and stared into the cup absentmindedly.

"A few weeks ago, I hired a new employee who supposedly had some good credentials. The Human Resources Department is expected to complete thorough background checks on all potential employees, but I just found out that one person was hired who was not qualified, a guy on my team. He lied on his resume about his education and experience. I checked with the university and learned he never earned a degree. He only took a couple of classes. In addition, one of his so-called former employers never heard of him. Another employer said he worked at his company for three months and quit. Apparently, one of the letters of recommendation was a forgery. Somehow, he got his hands on company stationery and proceeded to write his own letter. This guy is deceptive to the core."

Carl paused to pour some coffee. Samson barked at the kitchen door so Carl let him out into the back yard where the dog began running back and forth entertaining himself with a ball. Carl resumed his place at the table.

"On top of that, I heard this morning that he was arrested on assault and battery charges. After spending the night in the hospital and a brief court appearance, he was released on $4,000 bail, according to today's paper. Someone at the hospital found my business card in his wallet, correctly assumed he worked for me, and as a courtesy call, phoned me to explain why he was not at work today. I was wondering why he hadn't phoned. Now I have to fire the guy and find a new employee for the advertising firm."

Cory paused before asking a pivotal question.

"Carl, did you have any clue that he was not what he claimed to be?"

"No, not at first. Some things are starting to make more sense now. He was awfully young to have the experience he supposedly had acquired. The real giveaway was he never generated any original ideas. He would just agree with whatever someone else proposed. Now I see he was nothing but a young, blond punk, an imposter."

Carl ate a few minutes in silence.

"There's another problem too. Today I discovered that somebody bugged my office. Someone has heard every conversation I have had with clients, my family, and even you. I called the police and contacted my lawyer. I suspect the same man that impersonated an advertising agent is the same guy who bugged the office. The police department is conducting an investigation right now, reviewing surveillance tapes from our security cameras and questioning other employees about what they might have seen or heard. That guy's phone records and text messages are also being scrutinized for evidence. I also wouldn't be surprised if he stole some ideas and sold them to other companies. What really worries me is when he finds out he's terminated, he might decide to turn vindictive."

Cory sat in silence, listening to the unimaginable unfold. Had Cameron been Carl's employee? Was he living here in Pittsburgh? That could explain why he showed up at the motel parking lot as well as the restaurant. However, one question was a major puzzlement. How could Cameron be free on bail after that act of violence? What kind of an idiotic, liberal judge lets a psycho like Cameron out on bail and back out into society where he can harm innocent girls? Had he really recovered so quickly and been discharged from the hospital or did he take the liberty of just walking out the front door on his own initiative unnoticed?

"Carl, I was wondering. Do you ever tell your coworkers where you live or give out your home phone?"

Carl looked a little puzzled. "No, why do you ask?"

"Oh, I just think it is a good idea to keep personal information away from colleagues. I am sorry you have to go to all this trouble for a new employee. I hope you get a good replacement." He paused. "Carl, I have to ask you something. By any chance was the name of that employee Cameron?"

Carl looked up from his plate a bit stunned.

"Yes, how did you guess that?"

"He's an acquaintance of a friend of mine. Apparently, he's bad news all around. If he should show up at the office again, you need to be cautious. As you read for yourself in the paper, he has violent tendencies."

"Thanks for telling me. I'll fire him over the phone and mail a formal letter of termination as well. I'll make sure the receptionist does not allow him to see me or anyone else. I'll call building security and let them know about this too to deny him admittance."

"Carl, excuse me, but I just realized I need to call someone. I'll be back in a few minutes."

As Cory walked into his bedroom, he started to break out in a cold sweat. He sat on the bed and took in a deep breath to regain his composure. The thought of Cameron stalking not only him but Clarice as well generated fear for her and anger in general for the invasion of privacy and the threat to their safety. Reaching for the phone, he forced himself to remain calm. While dialing Clarice's number, he reminded himself that this was no time to display his rage against Cameron that was slowly building up inside him. Recognizing his lack of self-control at that moment, he silently chastised himself and focused on devising a plan of action to avoid problems with Cameron or confront them, if necessary. There was no answer, so he left a message.

"Clarice, Cory here. Listen, Cameron is out of the hospital and out on bail and sweetheart, there is something else. Cameron is living here in Pittsburgh working for my roommate, so he is around here somewhere. Please take extra precautions. Please don't go out at night alone. I am worried about you. Call me as soon as you can. Bye."

Cory walked back upstairs and resumed his place at the dinner table. Instead of eating, Carl was jotting down notes in his daily planner.

Ten minutes later, Cory's phone rang. He ran downstairs and sighed with relief when he heard Clarice's voice on the other end.

"Clarice, where are you?"

"Home. I was out shopping for a few groceries, but I am in now for the evening. I got your message. I can't believe this is happening. It's like a nightmare. I knew he was not emotionally stable, but now he resorts to lies to get a job in the same town that I'm in. He's scary. Why does he have to act like I am the only girl on the planet?"

Cory could hear the tension in her voice rising. The thought of her crying was unbearable.

"Clarice, come by the zoo this weekend, Saturday around ten. I'll be working with the cubs and I can arrange for you to see them. Would you like that?"

"Yes, I would actually."

"Great. Don't wear your good clothes. Jeans and a sweatshirt are fine. When working with the cubs, sometimes things can get a bit messy, but believe me this is an experience you will never forget."

CHAPTER 8

*S*aturday morning, chatting with Clarice over a couple of sodas was a delightful break from the morning paperwork. The zoo's snack bar sold sandwiches, chips, and cookies, a casual atmosphere not nearly as fancy as Sarafino's, but adequate for a quick bite. Clarice seemed calm and focused on their conversation as if Cameron were no longer a looming threat. Cory concluded that spending the afternoon with the lion cubs might cheer Clarice up and restore some normalcy to their relationship at the same time.

"Cory, thanks for bringing me here. This was a quiet place to eat. No interruptions. I needed to unwind."

Cory reached across the table and held her hand. Her green eyes brightened. She curled her fingers around his and squeezed his hand gently.

"Clarice, I have to say something. I hate to bring this up, but you have to move on with your own life. Cameron can't be allowed to keep on intimidating you. To be on the safe side, please contact the police. Report these incidents and put a restraining order on him."

Clarice sighed. "You're right. I have to do that. He has given me no choice."

"Thank you. I won't worry quite so much now. Well, since we are finished with lunch, would you like to see the cubs?"

Clarice's countenance glowed instantly.

"Yes, let's go."

"First, I have to get their formula. I made up some extra bottles yesterday so they are all ready. You can feed one of the cubs, if you like."

After retrieving the formula from the refrigerator, they walked into the enclosure. Clarice smiled at the two cubs sleeping in the sun.

"They are so little and so sweet. How adorable!"

Upon hearing Clarice's voice, Justin got up, stretched, and began prancing around the enclosure.

"Are you showing off for the lady, Justin? Are you letting her see how big and strong you are? He's marking off his territory again. It's a small kingdom, but he wants everyone to know that he rules it," said Cory with a grin.

Clarice laughed and sat down in a chair beside Cory. Jezebel stretched, yawned, swayed a moment to gain her balance, and stood up. When she saw the bottle, she headed in their direction, expecting to be fed.

"Here she comes. Clarice, you can pick her up and hold her or you can let her sit on the floor. She will drink either way."

"I feel nervous about picking her up. I'm afraid I might not hold her right. I'll let her just sit."

As Clarice held the bottle, Jezebel sat at her feet, gently wrapped one paw around the side of the bottle and began to drink. Meanwhile, Justin finished his circuit about the enclosure and watched Clarice intently as Jezebel drank.

"She is just too cute. How could anyone look at such an innocent looking kitten and give it a name like Jezebel, that horrible biblical villain? She should be named something that fits her beauty and gentleness like 'Princess.' That would suit you, wouldn't it, sweetheart? That's a better name for a pretty girl like you, isn't it?" said Clarice as she gently stroked the top of Jezebel's head.

Cory looked at Clarice. "Biblical villain? You read the Bible?"

Clarice nodded. "Yes, my godfather was a Methodist minister. My parents raised me on Bible verses. I got Bible stories each morning with my Cheerios, if you know what I mean. Now that I am back in Pittsburgh, I thought about attending my former church, the one I attended as a kid, but I haven't made up my mind yet."

"Maybe we can attend a service together sometime."

"Yes, I would like that."

After sitting in the sun a few minutes, Justin came over to Cory for his bottle. Cory put on the leather gloves, raised him gently, straddled the cub across his lap, and fed him.

"There you go, love. You enjoy that lunch. It's good for you," said Cory in soft tones.

As always, Justin grabbed the bottle firmly in both paws and tugged on it. Any time Cory spoke to Justin, the cat looked him in the eyes. The bonding process was progressing slowly, a little more each day. When he finished, Cory massaged his sides and then held the cub against his chest and shoulder, caressing him soothingly. Justin lay there, eyes shut, totally engrossed in the experience. A few minutes later, Jezebel finished drinking.

"Now it is time for Jezebel to get massaged. Do you want to try?"

"Well, yes, I think I should. I'll get the gloves first."

Modeling Cory's approach, Clarice bent over, carefully lifted Jezebel, laid her across her lap, removed the gloves, and massaged her gently. The cub lay there motionless, delighted to be getting more attention.

"Are you two enjoying yourselves?" The voice came from behind.

Cory turned to see Daniel standing in the doorway.

"Hi, Daniel. Clarice, this is my boss, Daniel Franklin. Daniel, this is my friend, Clarice. She wanted to see the cubs and interact with them today. Both of them finished up another bottle, so now they're getting another massage."

"Wonderful. Nice to meet you, Clarice. I hope you can come back and visit again sometime. Social interaction is good for the cubs. It is also important that they get their regular meals. Thanks for helping out."

"My pleasure. This is fun. I never thought I would get this close to a lion. She is so sweet," said Clarice as she stroked Jezebel's soft, tan fur. As she interacted with Jezebel, the cub began to respond more readily to her voice, displaying trust in Clarice's gentle hands. The cub breathed deeply for a few minutes, before deciding it was time to get down.

CARESSING LIONS

Both cubs began to squirm, so Clarice and Cory put the cubs down on the floor. Immediately, both of them headed for the spot under the skylight to sleep in the sun. Once again, Jezebel began to wash Justin's face and then her own.

"Cory, there's a friend of yours here today," said Daniel, stepping to one side. A photographer stepped into the enclosure followed by Carl.

"Hey, Cory. Daniel said this would be a good time to photograph the cubs for the advertisements. We talked it over and decided it would be best to take a few other pictures to use for brochures as well as posters to sell in the giftshop."

"The cubs are sleeping together right now. That will make a cute photo," said Cory, pointing in the direction of the cubs on the floor.

Carl made a gesture to the photographer to be very quiet. After getting out the camera equipment, Carl and the photographer walked toward the cubs. The photographer snapped a few photos, while Carl whispered a few suggestions on camera angles to maximize the use of the natural lighting. The cubs never stirred, napping peacefully. Afterward, Carl and the photographer went back to the other side of the room to let them sleep.

"Did you get some good shots?" asked Daniel, entering the enclosure with two extra chairs for Carl and the photographer.

Carl looked back at the sleeping cubs.

"Yes, they're just two big kittens in so many ways. If they don't nap too long, I would like to hang around and get some shots of them walking around. It would be better to have a variety of photos for the ad campaign."

"Actually, if you stay about another half hour, they will be up walking around again. They nap intermittently all day in short intervals. Nighttime is when they sleep the most," Cory explained.

Carl sat down and took a good look at Clarice. Cory noticed.

"Carl, I guess it is time for some introductions. This is my friend, Clarice. She's helping out today with the cubs. Clarice, this is my friend and roommate, Carl."

The two exchanged greetings. Before Carl had a chance to speak with Clarice, Cory asked, "And who is your photographer?"

"Cory, this is Wayne Anderson. He just started working for me last month, but he is very experienced. He's worked for newspapers in Philadelphia and Boston over the years and came highly recommended."

"Hi, Mr. Anderson. Thank you for your help and your interest in this project," said Cory.

Mr. Anderson looked about forty-five years old, with dark hair mixed with smatterings of gray. He smiled at Cory and Clarice.

"This is an unusual assignment for me. I've never had the chance to work with animals before, but I am glad I could take on this project."

Clarice sat watching the cubs. "Look, they're getting up again."

Carl turned his attention on the cubs, while Wayne got out his camera and selected a lens. At the same time, Justin stretched and walked to the other side of the enclosure looking out through a glass wall. He noticed a bird that had landed on a patch of grass and sat there watching it, spellbound by the new experience. Jezebel stretched and walked over beside her sibling to investigate what he had discovered. Wayne took several photos of them sitting together in the sunlight. In one shot, he even included the bird in the background. Cory sat their wondering if the cats' hunting instincts were emerging.

Daniel, who had momentarily left, returned with a tray of hot tea and sandwiches and set them down on the table. He seemed pleased with how Wayne and Carl carefully photographed the cubs, keeping their distances, so the cubs felt free to roam about.

"Gentlemen, here's some lunch for you, when you're ready."

After about ten minutes of taking photos, the two men returned to the table and helped themselves to the food.

"Thanks, Daniel. I was wondering when Wayne and I would have time for lunch. Our schedule is packed today."

The two men sat in silence, taking advantage of their only chance to eat, while Cory and Daniel quietly explained the ad campaign to Clarice.

"Well, we have all the shots we need. I will email some sample layouts to you, so you can choose which ones you prefer. Nice meeting you, Clarice. Cory, see you at dinner tonight," said Carl.

The two men left with their equipment and headed for a van in the guest parking lot.

"I hope this ad campaign draws more visitors to the zoo. That will help increase our revenue and raise awareness of the need to protect wildlife," said Daniel, sounding hopeful. After this first encounter with lions, Clarice became more intrigued with the project. To her surprise, after spending only a half hour with the cubs, she experienced a bond forming.

"Daniel, I work for a local newspaper. I was thinking the cubs and their development would make an interesting story," said Clarice.

"That's perfect. I am hoping to reach out to kids about wildlife preservation and perhaps educate another generation about the need to preserve and safeguard the animals. I'd like to encourage more school field trips to the zoo with a short presentation on lions and other jungle cats and include some kind of activities."

"I like that idea," Cory answered. "We should think of some small free things to give the kids and offer some merchandise that the school systems could use to expand the topic further in the classroom."

"Great. You come up with a list of ideas for ancillary materials for grade school teachers and then we will sit down and discuss the options."

Daniel headed back to his office. He was more than delighted with the way every aspect of the advertising campaign was progressing.

"I'm glad you could come by today, Clarice. I'm afraid I have to get back to work. I usually have a long list of emails waiting for me. I also have to type up some reports on the cats and their progress and get started brainstorming ideas for the school materials."

"I need to go too and start writing an article on the cubs. Thanks for letting me come, Cory."

"How about I call you sometime next week? We'll figure out something to do that we both enjoy. How does that sound?"

"Perfect. Next Saturday's my birthday."

"In that case, we will do something extra special."

As Clarice headed for the main entrance, Cory reassured himself about his first impressions of her. She was indeed tenderhearted, amiable, and outgoing. The perfect girlfriend for him. Still, one question remained: What was the best way to keep her safe from Cameron?

CHAPTER 9

*F*illed with excitement and anticipation, Cory called Clarice with great news. He prayed she would pick up the phone, so he would not have to leave a message.

"Clarice, hi. I'll bet you can't guess what I got you for your birthday?"

Clarice thought a moment, acting a little coy. "A picture frame?"

"No, something unique."

"A monogramed necklace?"

"No, think big."

"A villa in Tangiers, a yacht in Monte Carlo?"

Cory laughed. "No, silly. I got us two tickets to a Steelers game with great seats on the lower level near the fifty-yard line. Can you believe it? It's this Saturday afternoon. I hope you're free."

"Yes, I'm free. I can't believe it! Heinz Field again at last. I haven't been to a game in years."

"I have more good news. I bought a second-hand car, so I can pick you up."

"That's perfect. I am so looking forward to this. Thank you again for inviting me."

"My pleasure. I'll pick you up around noon. Take care. Bye."

On Saturday, the two of them drove to the stadium in Cory's white Ford Fiesta. It was sunny but rather cold for sitting outdoors, so Cory bought both of them matching Steelers sweatshirts.

"This extra layer of warmth is exactly what I needed. Thanks, Cory."

"If you're comfortable, I'm content." He kissed her gently on the cheek. Entering the stadium, they were pleasantly surrounded by energized fans. Almost every available seat was taken. As they maneuvered through the rows, vendors shouted out their wares, ranging from clothing to pizza and cold drinks. "It looks like a sell-out!" said Cory, overjoyed to witness the devotion of so many football enthusiasts.

As they sat in the stands and watched the game, crowds cheered as the Steelers advanced the ball against their formidable opponents, the Ravens. Steelers fans had made a huge turnout that day, an ocean of optimism overflowing in all directions. Steelers fans waved banners in the air and shouted, "We are victorious," as if some prognosticator had already proclaimed a magnanimous win for Pittsburgh. The hysteria of the fans was mounting. In Pittsburgh, football season was always like a sugar high coupled with an adrenaline rush. Everyone was happy and hyper like kids living on a steady diet of ice cream. After having won the Super Bowl numerous times, Steelers fans were always hopeful for another victory to keep the team's ranking in the upper echelons.

The afternoon sun shone on the stadium as the Steelers held the Ravens at the scrimmage line for two plays in a row. With third down and ten to go, the Ravens threw a pass. All of a sudden, half the stadium stood up screaming. A Steelers player intercepted the ball and took off for the end zone without a Ravens team member anywhere near him.

"Go, go! Look at him run," yelled the man sitting beside Cory.

The shouts and screams were deafening. Clarice stared at the player advancing down the field amazed by his speed and skill as the Ravens, who suddenly found themselves playing defense, scrambled in a futile attempt to tackle the Steelers man.

"An interception coupled with a touchdown. My kind of game," said Cory as a Steelers player danced a moment in the end zone.

He hugged Clarice and then took off his gloves to eat some more popcorn.

The man sitting behind them, wearing a Steelers knit cap and scarf, jumped up screaming, "Yes! That's my team! We're number one! Steelers: more powerful than eighteen-wheelers!"

Cory laughed quietly, and said to Clarice, "My boss's father is a truck driver. He'd love to hear a cheer like that."

The fan obviously felt as intensely passionate about football the same way the little kids in the stadium felt about the word "mother." By the end of the game, the Steelers had beaten the Ravens thirty to twelve. A memorable event complete with hot dogs, popcorn, and a few selfies.

As they walked back to the car, Cory said, "Clarice, my aunt has invited us for Thanksgiving dinner. I told her I had a friend I wanted to bring along and she is fine with that. Would you like to come? I'd love for you to meet her." He realized that was an understatement.

"I'll have to check with my folks to see if they mind. I think they were counting on us being together as a family. If I spend the day with you, I'll need to make it up to them somehow like extra days at Christmas and New Year's Day. Let me talk with them first."

"Sure. You can let me know later. Would you like to go somewhere for coffee or something else to eat? It's almost five thirty."

"That's a good idea. Let's go to a coffee shop and chat a little more. I'm not ready to go home just yet." As they left the stadium, they passed a number of cars with bumper stickers that read "Steelers: Victory Awaits" and "Steelers Fan: Pennsylvania Proud."

About twenty minutes later they arrived at Coffee Bar Roasters. Immediately upon opening the door, the intense aromas of various coffees bombarded their senses. A long display case of various sandwiches and pastries stood on the right side of the room. On the left, rows of coffee mugs, coffee makers, and bags of imported coffees lined several shelves.

"Carl and I came here a few nights ago to hang out and talk. I thought you would like it here, especially since it has a fireplace." Cory glanced at the menu on the wall and the desserts arranged esthetically in front of him. Cory loved sweets, but after the quantity of treats consumed at the game, he decided against ordering a donut.

"That is just what I need. I am going to grab a table over there right by the fire."

"Two medium black coffees, a newspaper, and two ham and cheese croissants please," said Cory to the cashier, who filled the order with a smile.

"Thank you, sir. Come again."

"That sure was an exciting game. The Steelers usually do well. If they could just start beating the New England Patriots on a regular basis, I would be sincerely happy," said Cory, as he sat down across from Clarice.

Clarice sat there still wearing her coat and gloves watching the fire.

"There you are, my dear, something to warm you up."

Clarice reached for the coffee and wrapped her hands around the sides of the cup to remove the chill from her fingers.

"Thank you. Between this and the fireplace, I think I can thaw out now," Clarice said, as she turned the chair sideways facing the fireplace and stretched her legs out.

"There's a sandwich for you. I'm going to check the sports page a second to see where the Steelers are playing their next game," said Cory, anticipating an exciting sport schedule.

Opening up the paper, Cory noticed an article on the front page.

"Clarice, listen to this. 'Yesterday, police picked up an intoxicated man in downtown Pittsburgh. The man, identified as twenty-six-year-old Cameron Dunkel, was walking into oncoming traffic and yelling for everyone to get out of his way. A number of vehicles swerved and barely missed colliding with other cars. One witness reported that a pedestrian attempted to guide the drunken man back onto the sidewalk. While screaming obscenities, Mr. Dunkel shoved the man to the pavement and continued staggering, alternating between walking on the sidewalk and in the street. Several onlookers called the police. Unidentified sources claim Mr. Dunkel was fined for public intoxication, jaywalking, reckless endangerment, and obstructing the flow of traffic."

Clarice closed her eyes and shook her head in total disgust.

"I'm not surprised. That's Cameron all over. Drunk and dying for attention any way he can get it. He infuriates me and yet part of me feels sorry for him. He never found his own purpose, his own sense of direction. Never finished college. He's smart. The frightening part is he can be diabolically clever. He's had good jobs in the past, but nothing seems to work out for him. He can actually be civil when he isn't drunk or broiling mad, but those times are scarce. He just can't figure out how life works. For some reason, he seems to want to live vicariously through me," Clarice said, glancing out the window at passing pedestrians.

"Did you ever put a restraining order on him?"

"Yes. I filed a report with the police department the same day I discussed the matter with you at the zoo. I can't have him showing up at work or at my apartment. He's too scary, too violent. I keep hoping that somehow, he will get some help. At this point, with a court order to stay away from me, I bet he won't bother me again."

"I wouldn't want to play against those odds in Vegas. I will never trust him to stay away. Clarice, never hesitate to call the police, if he shows up."

Clarice sat in silence, gazing into the flames in the ornate gas fireplace. It reminded her of the comforts of home surrounded by family.

"By the way, did you finish the article on the cubs? I'm looking forward to reading it."

"Yes, it's coming out in tomorrow's edition. I think you'll like it. I got a couple good pictures of the cubs playing. If the editor-in-chief wants me to write a follow up story, I'd love to come back, take more pictures, and interview you and Mr. Franklin. I'm also thinking about a special newspaper insert for children with pictures, a puzzle, a quiz, and place to draw."

"I bet the kids would love something like that. If you do write another story on the cats, don't hesitate to call the office. Daniel and I would be glad to assist you with setting up a meeting."

"When will Carl's posters and ads be coming out?"

"Soon. He's finishing them right now. He mentioned that at dinner the other night."

Clarice sat up and unwrapped the croissant sandwich.

"Cory, where does your aunt live?"

"About an hour north of here. Why?"

"Well, one way or the other, I definitely want to be out of town for Thanksgiving. I don't want Cameron to have a chance of running into me. I want to get out of here."

"You are more than welcome to join me. You know that."

He reached across the table and held her hand.

"Let me check with my folks. It does sound like a good plan," she said, smiling.

She leaned over and kissed him.

CHAPTER 10

Cory's aunt, Evelyn Baker, lived in a modest stone house about an hour outside of Pittsburgh. Her husband had died about five years previously, but she continued to live there in a home filled with blissful memories. An American flag was mounted on a support beam by the front steps to honor veterans like her father who had fought in WWII. Overall, the house looked manicured. Green shutters were mounted by the front windows. White flower boxes were attached to each window on both levels. Clarice tried to imagine what the façade would look like in spring with various flowers blooming. In addition, matching rattan furniture welcomed visitors to rest on the front porch. As Cory and Clarice walked up to the house, Cory pointed to a rocking chair.

"Her husband bought her that for their twentieth wedding anniversary. That's all she wanted along with her husband to talk to. You're going to like her. She is a sweet soul."

Evelyn opened the door with a smile, eyes shining.

"Cory, I can't believe it's you. It's been three years. You look wonderful. This must be Clarice. Oh, Cory, she's lovely. Come in, come in!"

"Good afternoon, Mrs. Baker. It's good to meet you. It was kind of you to invite us over for dinner," said Clarice cordially.

"Clarice, if there is one thing I love, it's company. You two make yourselves at home here in the living room, while I put a few finishing touches on the table."

Cory and Clarice sat down and looked about the room. The place looked like a user-friendly museum with hand-painted vases from Japan, an oil painting of the Swiss Alps, photographs of Bavarian castles, carved elephants from India, a Waterford crystal serving bowl, and a silver plate with a copper etching in the middle with the word "Jerusalem" at the bottom.

"She traveled quite a bit with her husband. They took numerous trips all over Europe and the Middle East together. All over the world. I think the rug is from China and I believe that crucifix is from Rome."

Evelyn returned and sat down with them.

"So, tell me. How did you two meet?"

"At a tent revival a few miles outside Titusville. This beautiful lady agreed to dance with me and we have been dating ever since," said Cory, giving Clarice an adoring look.

Clarice sat there, smiling, feeling like sunken treasure that someone had finally discovered.

"That's wonderful. My late husband and I met at an art auction. We were admiring the same painting. He outbid me on the picture. Afterward, he felt guilty and invited me to dinner. We were married two years later. Of course, from that moment on, I owned that painting too."

Clarice laughed. "What a wonderful story. Cory and I have had some interesting times together going out to eat, attending football games, and even playing with lions."

"What? Lions? Cory, you told me on the phone you got a job at the zoo, but I hope it's not dangerous," said Evelyn, a little disconcerted.

"It's okay, Aunt Evelyn. They are only cubs. Clarice and I bottle fed them a couple weeks ago. I'll have to send you some pictures of them."

"Cory, did you know your Uncle Joseph went on a lion safari with me for our tenth anniversary?"

Cory sat there silent a moment, pleasantly surprised.

"No, I didn't. Where did you go?"

"Kenya. Let me show you a picture I took."

She stepped into the next room and brought back a large framed photo of Uncle Joseph with a lioness and two cubs in the background about thirty yards away.

"We took that picture fast, just in case the lioness got agitated. Isn't that a nice shot? I guess a love for lions runs in the family."

Cory studied the picture carefully. As best he could tell, the cubs in the photo were about as old as Justin and Jezebel, lying in the sun, protected by their mother. For a moment, he was saddened to think that his cubs would be confined to a zoo and never roam around in the wild, but then again, at least at the zoo they were safe and cared for, since they had no mother of their own.

"Oh, aren't they adorable? What a fantastic picture. What a unique experience," said Clarice.

"Yes, it was. Probably the best vacation we ever had, although we took many memorable trips together," said Evelyn.

She paused to look at the photo as if resurrecting past images in her mind of time spent with Joseph. He had been the love of her life and no one could ever take his place.

"Well, dinner is ready, so let's eat, shall we?"

Looking at the table beautifully spread with all the trimmings, Cory realized how much he missed homecooked meals. Turkey, mashed potatoes, homemade gravy, sausage stuffing, green beans with almonds, and salad. A crystal vase filled with various flowers boasting fall colors crowned the center of the table. Two candlesticks made of hand-carved olive wood from Israel stood on either side of the vase.

"Aunt Evelyn, I have to ask you something. Have you spoken with my parents about me?"

"No, dear. I haven't said a word. If you want to tell them anything, that is up to you. I don't want to interfere." Cory's instincts served him well. Inside, all along, he knew he could trust her.

"Thanks. Now that I'm settled and had a chance to think things through I'll probably call them this weekend. Life feels so much better being on my own."

"Clarice, Cory tells me you're a journalist. What kind of articles have you written?"

"Well, I've interviewed the mayor and some football players. I also wrote an article on the lion cubs that Cory works with at the zoo. That was an interesting assignment. I also write editorials on issues that concern Pittsburgh in general."

The three of them chatted for over an hour sharing stories and enjoying extra helpings of everything on the table. Evelyn's home reminded Cory of Paul's cabin, a retreat far away from the rest of the world, a microcosm of society thriving as its own entity with only one maxim: Relax and enjoy yourself.

"Be sure and save room for dessert. I baked four pies: pumpkin, blueberry, apple, and peach."

"Aunt Evelyn, why would you bake four pies for three people?"

"I want to be sure that you two get at least one slice of something you love," said Evelyn enthusiastically.

"In that case, I am not eating another bite to save room for a slice of peach pie," said Clarice with a smile.

"You are both welcome to take leftovers home with you when you go. That way you won't have to worry about cooking for a few days."

"Thanks, Aunt Evelyn. That is so sweet of you."

After they had finished eating, Cory insisted that he clear the table and load the dishwasher, while Clarice and his aunt sat and relaxed. Evelyn was indeed the perfect hostess. Now it was time for her to take a turn at feeling like a guest.

"Why don't we enjoy our pie on the front porch with some coffee?" Evelyn asked.

"I never turn down pie, Aunt Evelyn, no matter where it's served. How about you and Clarice sit out front and chat and I'll serve the pie and coffee," said Cory.

After making their dessert selections, Evelyn smiled at Clarice and the two of them headed out to the porch, while putting on their jackets. Clarice sat on the porch swing to make sure Evelyn had a chance to sit on her favorite rocker. The late afternoon sky was bright blue with streaks of white clouds as delicate as an artist's brushstrokes.

"Cory is such a kind, young man. He's my favorite nephew. So considerate."

"You're right; he is. He is always thinking of things he can do for me," said Clarice as she swayed gently on the white porch swing.

Cory appeared with a small folding table, which he set up between the two women. He returned a moment later with three servings of pie and then the coffee.

"I think I got your orders straight. If you want a slice of something else, just ask. I'll get it."

Delightful conversation ensued. Cory divulged his accounts of meeting Paul Jamison and Mr. Franklin, his boss's father. Clarice talked about her new apartment, the sites of Pittsburgh, and her most recent articles. Likewise, Aunt Evelyn shared stories of growing up in the 1960s and travels with her husband.

An hour later, Evelyn packaged up the promised leftovers. She gave Clarice an entire blueberry pie to take home for her and her roommate. Cory gladly took the remaining slices of apple pie to share. As they were loading up the car with the food, Cory's cell phone rang.

"Cory, I just called to tell you to be extra cautious when you come home tonight. You're not going to believe this."

"Carl, what are you talking about?"

"Someone set fire to the front porch. I was in the kitchen, when the dog started barking incessantly. I went into the living room to see what was wrong and saw the flames from the front window. I called the police and the fire department. The damage is not too extensive, but I'll have to replace some boards and get the porch repainted. It would have been worse, if I hadn't been home. Cory, this guy was crazy drunk, swearing his lungs out."

"Did you get a good look at him?"

"Yes, it was Cameron Dunkel, the guy I fired. Somehow, he found out where I live. Remember when I mentioned my office was bugged? He probably heard me mention my address during a personal call to a doctor when I made an appointment. I guess this is his revenge for getting canned. When I came to the window, he was swearing and saying your name, then he saw me, turned, and ran down the walkway. He took off in a blue sports car. The police are looking for him right now. Cameron knows that both of us live here. I'm convinced he's the one who bugged the phone in my office, when I was out doing the ad campaign for the zoo. I inadvertently left my office unlocked that morning. That was his opportunity to get inside. Maybe he hacked into my computer too. We can talk later. Just be careful coming home, okay?"

"I will, Carl. Thanks for letting me know."

As the two of them got into the car, Cory turned to Clarice, relaying the conversation he had with Carl. Clarice sighed and shook her head.

"He's ruining my life and now he's ruining yours. I can't take it!" shouted Clarice as tears formed in her eyes.

Cory leaned over and hugged Clarice. She was shaking and breathing heavily.

"I'm right here. The important thing now is to have a plan. I don't think it's safe to go home tonight. I know my aunt will let us stay here for the weekend. It will give the police a chance to track him down without him knowing where we are. She has several guestrooms. We can take the food back into the house and store it in her freezer in the basement. To be safe, call your roommate and tell her to keep the apartment locked up tight and watch out for anyone lurking around the building. I'll phone Carl and tell him what we're doing so he won't worry. There's no telling what Cameron might try next. It sounds like he is losing his mind."

"This has to stop," Clarice cried, holding onto Cory.

"It will, sweetheart. I don't know how, but it will."

All of a sudden, Clarice sat upright and looked into Cory's eyes.

"If he knows where you live, he might also know where you work."

Clarice's eyes widened and she gasped.

"Oh no, Cory. The cubs!"

CHAPTER 11

*A*fter consuming a hearty meal with the company of his family, Daniel headed down to the zoo to check in on the cubs and give them an afternoon feeding. Since Cory had taken the day off and other volunteers were out of town, Daniel assumed the responsibility of caring for the cats. While walking across the parking lot, he noticed smoke rising from the landscaped area near the entrance. He stared in disbelief. The bushes and lawn near his office were on fire and the flames were beginning to spread to the flowerbeds and other greenery.

At once, he notified the fire department and quickly headed for the lion enclosure, the closest structure to the flames. As Daniel opened the door, he saw the cubs cowering in a corner, trembling. They could see the bushes on fire through the glass wall at one end of their room. Instinctively fearing an assault on their safety as the flames rose and the smell of smoke increased, the cubs cried incessantly. Trying to find a way out of the enclosure, Justin clawed at the wall and floor and Jezebel attempted to bury her head in Justin's side in a feeble attempt to comfort herself.

As the firetruck pulled up outside and began extinguishing the blaze, Daniel sat on the floor and held the two cubs, stroking them and talking to them softly. "It's okay, sweethearts. I'm here. You're safe now. Take it easy." The cubs responded to Daniel's gentle touch and soothing sounds of his voice as they nuzzled against him and gradually quieted down.

As a precautionary measure, Daniel moved the cubs to a room at the end of the hall away from the flames. When faced with these strange surroundings filled with furniture, the cubs cried initially but slowly began exploring their new environment. It was not a perfect place for them, but at least they were out of immediate danger. Due to a quick response, the firefighters put out the flames within less than ten minutes. After being informed that the fire was out and the danger was past, Daniel carefully lifted each cub and returned the cats to their enclosure. They were still agitated, so he spoke to them softly, gently stroking their heads. About twenty minutes later, Daniel managed to coax the cats to drink their formula. Finally, after eating, the cubs resumed their naps in their straw beds.

As Daniel stood up to leave, the phone rang. The person on the other end began speaking the moment he lifted the receiver.

"Daniel, it's Cory. I have to warn you about something." Cory began informing Daniel of the horrific incidents at Carl's house and the restaurant, along with a description of the blue sports car and a physical description of Cameron. Daniel listened, noting every detail.

"Thanks for contacting me. I just had to contact the fire department about a fire by the front entrance. It's out now and the animals are safe. I'll have the police review the footage from the security cameras to see if we can identify the culprit," said Daniel.

"So the cubs are safe?" asked Cory, seeking some reassurance.

"Yes, they're fine. They were scared to death, but they calmed down, drank their formula, and went to sleep," said Daniel calmly.

The horrific image of that maniac harming the lions overwhelmed Cory.

"I'll contact the police and request extra security around here for at least the next couple of weeks. As you know, we have security cameras and alarm systems, but this requires extra precautions, since we are dealing with an arsonist," said Daniel.

"I'm so sorry to bother you on a holiday, but I knew you would want to be aware of this. I'm out of town for the weekend, but I plan on coming in to work on Monday. If anything changes, I will let you know."

Cory hung up the phone and held Clarice. She broke down and sobbed. Cory just sat quietly and held her. For the moment, there was nothing else to do.

On Sunday afternoon, Cory and Clarice drove back toward Pittsburgh, relieved that they had enjoyed a few quiet days to talk without interruption and had put some distance between themselves and Cameron's insanity and sadistic schemes. Evelyn gave them some space for private conversations, but she was also there to listen as they shared their struggles and potential solutions.

"Clarice, what we really need to do now is be careful. The police have been notified and have assured us they will keep vigilant and patrol our neighborhoods. We can't let Cameron rule our lives or else he wins this war."

For a while, they drove along in silence, while Cory thought about another outing that they could enjoy. He was trying to do anything to keep her mind off Cameron.

"Clarice, let's take a boat ride, a site-seeing tour on the Alleghany this Saturday. There is a snack bar onboard, so we can have a light lunch and enjoy the day. According to the weather report, it should be sunny. How does that sound? Just the two of us."

Clarice was quiet a moment and then said, "Yes, I would like that. Out on the water it will feel like we are in a different world. We can have some space."

"How about I pick you up around nine forty-five. I'll make reservations for us and call you tomorrow with more details. Bring a jacket. It will be rather windy on the water."

"Good idea. I am looking forward to this, Cory."

As they drove along the interstate, Cory heard a loud engine revving up behind them. In the rearview mirror, Cory saw a speeding car, trying to pass on a double yellow line. He couldn't believe it, but there was Cameron barreling along at top speed. Cory recognized the blue Stingray.

In an authoritative voice, Cory said, "Clarice, get out your cell phone. Call the police. Give them our location and tell them Cameron Dunkel is tracking us." While making the suggestion, Clarice quickly got her phone out, calling 911, talking with a dispatcher, providing details.

Moving into the left lane, Cameron roared the motor and began driving parallel with Cory's Fiesta. Glaring at the two of them, hatred erupting in his eyes, Cameron screamed obscenities.

"God, help us. I don't believe this," said Clarice shocked and frightened.

All of a sudden, to avoid a head on collision, Cameron hit the brakes and moved back into the right lane behind Cory. The driver in the left lane drove by the blue sports car yelling with his fist in the air and blasting his horn. Several more cars passed from the opposite direction.

"He's drunk again. I just know it. Please be careful, Cory."

Cory hoped Cameron would come to his senses, but once more Cameron raced ahead, pulling alongside Cory in the left lane, driving parallel to his Ford.

"Clarice, he's going to ram us. Brace yourself and hang on."

Grabbing the handgrip above the door and tightening her seatbelt, Clarice held her breath, shut her eyes and prayed, "Please, God, get us out of this."

Looking into the rearview mirror, Cory realized no one was behind him. As Cameron was getting ready to swerve into them, Cory slammed on the brakes, tires screeching. A second later, Cameron made a sharp turn of the wheel moving into the right lane, missing the white Ford by inches. Cameron's car swerved, swayed from side to side and centered itself again on the road. With a look of disgust in the rearview mirror, shaking his fist, Cameron sped on ahead and out of sight.

"That was close. Good maneuver, Cory. That saved our lives," said Clarice as she tried to breathe normally again.

"The thought just came to me out of nowhere. Thank you, Lord, for the inspiration," said Cory, feeling calmer.

"I wonder if it was a coincidence or if he trailed us. He seems to know your car," said Clarice, still shaken from the experience.

"Apparently, we have to be on guard all the time. You were right. He does have a way of showing up where you least expect him."

For the next five days, the only thing that really kept Cory from worrying about Clarice was the relaxation he found working with Justin and Jezebel. They were growing from all the formula and becoming stronger. More importantly, they were bonding more closely with Cory and Daniel. Both cubs displayed their affection more openly and responded to the two men's voices when called. Cory felt more like a parent every day.

As much as Cory loved working with the cats, he knew the day would come when he could no longer hold them and make them feel secure. That sense of separation anxiety saddened him. He knew he would miss them, but in the meantime, he would live in the moment and enjoy whatever time he could spend with them. Even though the cubs were precious, what mattered most in his life was Clarice. He knew now what he felt was more than mere infatuation. He loved her and would do anything to protect her.

CHAPTER 12

On Saturday morning, Clarice and Cory arrived at the boat dock. Boyhood memories of traveling down the river with his father filled Cory's mind and he reminded himself of the necessary phone call he had to make to his parents. He wanted to feel like part of a family again.

"I already have the tickets so let's get onboard. The boat departs at ten thirty," Cory said excitedly as he walked along with Clarice hand in hand to the boat.

"I found out the ride lasts only one hour so we can think of something else to do later on, if you want."

The ship was called *The Gateway Clipper* and boasted several decks for viewing the cityscape. The main deck featured a large enclosed space for dining at a snack bar as well as additional indoor seating. Eager for good seats, Cory and Clarice headed to the top deck to get to the highest vantage point.

"We should get a great view of the city from here," said Cory, admiring the beauty of the river as it curved around the city's skyscrapers.

"You know, as often as I have spent time downtown, this is one thing I have never done. I guess I didn't want to feel like a tourist, but then again, why should they have all the fun, right?" said Clarice, laughing.

In a few minutes, the boat pulled away from the dock. The breeze was brisk but in the sunshine, the two of them sat comfortably.

"I'm glad you suggested I bring my jacket. It would be too cold out here without it," said Clarice.

They sat next to each other on outside benches, holding hands, and enjoying the scenery. As the ship navigated down the river, the captain narrated a brief history of Pittsburgh about its origins as a village and how it gradually expanded into a metropolis. The captain also pointed out several buildings of interest and other historical developments of the city. After about thirty minutes of cruising on the river, Clarice looked totally relaxed.

"Are you enjoying yourself?" Cory asked.

Sitting with her head tipped back, picking up the sun's morning rays, Clarice smiled and said, "Yes, this is fabulous. What a terrific way to relax."

Her red hair glowed in the bright sunlight.

"How about I go downstairs and get us some sandwiches and coffee? Sound good?"

"Sounds perfect."

Cory leaned over and kissed her. "You stay here and I'll be right back as soon as I can."

He kissed her again and headed downstairs.

Clarice sat on the bench, eyes shut, enjoying the warmth of the sun on her face and the breeze. As she rested, she thought for a moment she might fall asleep. Without a doubt, this was the perfect outing. For the next five minutes, her mind drifted off to memories of Cory on Evelyn's front porch and the joy she felt feeding the lion cub.

"Are you enjoying your trip?" a passerby asked.

"Oh, yes. Definitely. This is so peaceful. I think…"

Clarice opened her eyes to find Cameron staring at her. Somehow, he had trailed them to the dock. Clarice could clearly see the remnants of a bruise on his forehead where Cory had smacked him with the frying pan.

"What are you doing here? How did you find me? Can't you just leave me in peace? Can't you get a life of your own?"

Clarice's voice grew gradually louder. Unfortunately, no other passengers were on the top deck who might have intervened with the confrontation.

"I don't want you spending time with him. You're my girl. You might not realize it yet, but that is who you are. Get that through your head!"

Cameron had a fierce look in his eyes, wild, untamed.

"I'll never be your girl. Never!" screamed Clarice.

At that moment, Cory appeared at the top of the stairs with the lunch tray. Upon seeing Cameron, Cory was shocked. In fact, for a split second he doubted the evidence in front of his eyes, but it was Cameron. Cory recognized his voice and the back of his blond head. Outraged, Cory set the tray down on the bench and came up to him silently from behind, hoping the element of surprise would put him at an advantage.

Clarice noticed Cory coming but kept her eyes on Cameron.

"If you aren't going to be with me, you aren't going to be with anybody!" Cameron screamed.

As Cory was about to pin Cameron's arm from behind and knock him senseless, Cameron seized Clarice by the neck and pushed her head backward halfway over the railing, squeezing her throat. Clarice gasped trying to take in air, while wrestling with his wrist to free herself. With his other hand, Cameron grabbed her under the knees and with one swift movement flipped her backward over the side of the boat.

Clarice let out a horrific scream as she fell over the side and plunged into the river.

Instinctively, Cory ran to the side of the railing, grabbed a life ring, and threw it into the water where he saw her go down, while yelling, "Man overboard!"

Darkness began to envelop Clarice as she sank lower. Her muscles tightened in the cold water. Her fingers and feet began to grow numb. Moving her arms and legs as vigorously as she could, she swam toward the surface, longing for air and sunlight. She thought her lungs would burst from not taking a breath, but the painful struggle to reach the top and preserve her life was worth it. Just as important to her, Cory was worth it.

Meanwhile, on the top deck, eyes blazing with anger, hot as a blowtorch, Cameron turned on Cory like an armed missile seeking a new target. Cameron launched himself at Cory, fists flying. Knowing how Cameron fought from the previous encounter, Cory delivered one intense blow to Cameron's jaw and a second one to the stomach. Cameron staggered backward and came at Cory again like a rabid dog, insane and mindless. Watching every move, Cory dodged Cameron's swing and struck him in the jaw again full force. Cameron, astounded at Cory's strength, stumbled backward toward the railing, lost his balance, and toppled over the side, arms and legs flailing in all directions.

Immediately, Cory threw a second life ring into the water to mark the spot where Cameron had fallen. Whether friend or foe, it was not part of Cory's nature to let someone die needlessly. Next, Cory kicked off his shoes and dove into the water. By this time, Clarice had managed to swim back to the surface, gasping for air, and hanging on to the life ring. As quickly as possible, Cory swam up alongside of her as she took in huge gulps of air and pushed her wet hair off her face. Her eyes were red and burning from pollutants in the river.

"You are going to be okay. I'm here," he said, putting his arm around her for a moment.

Looking in the direction where Cameron had fallen, Cory scanned the area. There was no sign of him, only the floating life ring. Fortunately, several other passengers witnessed three people going over the side and notified the captain who immediately turned the boat around.

As the boat pulled up alongside of them, a crew member reached for Cory. He shook his head. "No, take her first," whereupon the man hoisted Clarice onboard, then pulled up Cory out of the water, wrapping both of them in towels.

"Was it just the two of you that fell in the water? Someone reported seeing three people go over the side," said a crew member.

Cory's emotions were divided. Part of him could not have cared less if Cameron drowned. He was a menace. A viper. Cory was quite tempted to deny anyone else was involved. However, his moral conscience could neither lie about the situation nor fabricate a tale in front of Clarice. She trusted him to do the right thing always. He would never deliberately break that confidence. He looked at a member of the first aid team.

"Yes, there was another person in the water."

Clarice gave the staff member Cameron's full name and a detailed account of what happened. Meanwhile, the captain radioed for assistance and continued the search. Ten minutes later he got a message that a sailboat had picked up a man from the water along with the details of time and location.

Cory held Clarice tightly, sitting on a bench inside the boat near the snack bar. A staff member had positioned them in front of a wall heater and had turned it on high.

"Thank God you kept your wits about you, held your breath, and swam to the surface. Some folks would have panicked in that situation and just gone straight down," said Cory, relieved.

Clarice looked directly into Cory's eyes.

"You were the reason I fought so hard to keep alive. As I fell into the water, I told myself 'It can't end like this' and I made sure it didn't. Thank you again for rescuing me."

"You are more than welcome."

He hugged her again and kissed her. Turning to a staff member, he asked, "Could you please bring two cups of hot coffee over here? By the way, there's a tray on the top deck with sandwiches. Could someone bring those down here? I don't want to go outdoors dripping wet in that wind."

A young teen attending the snack bar jumped to her feet and brought the coffee. She smiled at the two of them.

"I'm glad you guys are all right. There's not much I can do for you I'm afraid, but I can do this much. I'll get that tray of food for you too."

Cory thanked her and handed Clarice one of the cups.

"I've never been so grateful for hot coffee in my whole life," said Cory, sipping the beverage.

"I don't understand this. It's like being trailed by a killer dog like in *The Hound of the Baskervilles*," said Clarice. "How did Cameron find out where we were?"

"Carl mentioned that his phone at the office had been bugged. Two weeks ago, I called Carl at work to chat and mentioned I was thinking about taking you here this weekend. That would explain it. Carl removed the listening device and handed it over to the police for safekeeping and criminal evidence. At least, Cameron can't eavesdrop anymore."

A side door opened and the snack bar attendant returned with the tray of sandwiches Cory had left behind on the upper deck. As Clarice and Cory sat there and ate, they reflected on this latest horrendous incident with Cameron.

"The first thing we have to do is get back to our own homes and get into some dry clothes, then later we can sit down and have a serious talk. I think we have had enough excitement for one day," said Cory.

"Definitely," answered Clarice.

For the next few minutes, they sat quietly eating, listening to the rumbling of the ship's engine, sipping coffee, and silently thanking God they had survived a potentially deadly ordeal at the hands of a maniac. As the late morning sunlight streamed through the windows on either side of the main level, the boat's captain walked into the enclosure and approached the couple, looking concerned.

Pulling up a chair alongside of them, he said, "Good morning. I'm Captain Nelson. I wanted to come by and see how you were doing."

He noticed the food and the towels.

"I trust the staff assisted you as best they could."

"Yes, sir. They have. We just need to get into some dry clothes," said Cory.

The captain sat down slowly next to them. His voice became more serious.

"I'm glad you made it onboard safely. However, I did want to tell you something. I didn't know if you had heard. According to an eyewitness on a sailboat, a man was picked up from the water. The two crewmen on board attempted CPR for twenty-five minutes but could not revive him. They identified the man from some ID he had in his wallet zipped up in a jacket pocket. It's the same name that you gave to the other crew member. I just thought I should let you know he didn't survive."

The air suddenly seemed still, thick, and difficult to inhale.

"Thank you for telling us, captain," Cory said in a somber tone.

"All the best to you both," said Captain Nelson as he rose and headed back upstairs to the bridge.

Clarice began to tear up. She leaned her head on Cory's shoulder and shuddered, taking in long, deep breaths.

"He's dead. That stupid jerk. Why did he have to act like this?" Clarice cried.

"I don't know. It's sad anytime someone dies young. This is tragic, Clarice, but as you know, he brought all of this on himself."

"I know," she responded quietly. "I know."

For the next twenty minutes as the boat returned to the dock, Cory held Clarice in silence. He knew that sometimes simply sitting beside someone was the best medicine for pain.

Around one o'clock that afternoon, Cory's Ford Fiesta pulled up in front of Clarice's brick apartment complex. For about a minute, Clarice sat there staring, focusing on nothing in particular but the end of the road, which appeared blurry through watery eyes. The morning's trauma had left her feeling numb and cold, inside and out. Cory leaned over and kissed her. Her lovely red hair, which usually cascaded down her shoulders with a bright shine, hung limp, filthy, and matted. Nevertheless, to Cory, she still looked beautiful. True love may be blind to outward appearances, but oftentimes, it can perceive the inner beauty of the soul with perfect clarity.

"Go on inside, sweetheart. This is the time for you to think about taking care of yourself," said Cory gently. "If you want to talk, call me."

She turned her head and looked him in the eyes for a moment. As if awakening from a hypnotic trance, she blinked a couple times and replied, "You're right. Thank you." Clarice took in a deep breath and sighed. She concentrated on pushing aside her depressed emotions and said assertively, "I'm going to toss these dirty clothes in the washing machine, get a hot shower, wash this grime out of my hair, put on a clean outfit, and take a nap. When I get up, I'm making myself a cup of Earl Grey." Concentrating on mundane tasks made her feel a little more normal. She paused, examining Cory's face closely.

"This is the third time you've been my hero," she said with a faint smile.

She leaned over and kissed him. Cory walked around to the passenger's side and opened the door for her. She gradually stood up and headed into the house. Cory waited until she closed the front door securely, before driving off.

That evening, Clarice received a phone call from her parents asking if she had heard about Cameron's passing. The agonizing irony of the question burned like hot acid on an open wound, as Clarice listened to how the neighborhood back home was reacting to Cameron's death. After retrieving the corpse from the fishing boat and verifying the identity of the body, the police had notified Mr. and Mrs. Dunkel that afternoon with the heartbreaking news. At the request of the family, the community association for the housing complex sent out the details of Cameron's tragic demise in a group email, which Mr. Lyons discovered after dinner as he browsed through a list of correspondence. Emotions rising to the surface once more, Clarice cried as she listened to her mother read the email. Trying to compose herself, Clarice longed for the time when all this excruciating pain would fade away.

As anticipated, the next day, Clarice and Cory each received phone calls from the police department requesting a meeting with the police chief, so the local authorities could file a report on the events onboard *The Gateway Clipper*. Upon entering the detective's office, they noticed the investigator's eyes expressed a look of concern for both of them.

"I spoke with Captain Nelson yesterday and he provided me with some basic information about where he found you and the condition you were both in when you were rescued from the river," the officer stated. "At this time, we need details of the incident regarding what led up to Mr. Dunkel's death and why you needed to be rescued."

Chronologically, Cory provided a full account of what had transpired, answering numerous questions, especially regarding the horrific moment when Cameron threw Clarice overboard. Likewise, with tremendous effort, Clarice painfully described the events to the investigator who took detailed notes, interjecting with an occasional question for clarification. Legal records, already on file, included a full report of Cameron's fist fight with Cory at Sarafino's, his drunken misconduct in downtown Pittsburgh, film footage verifying one account of arson at the Pittsburgh Zoo, a second account of arson at a private residence based on Carl Christianson's phone call to emergency dispatch, one account of wiretapping in Mr. Christianson's office, one account of stalking and reckless endangerment on the freeway based on Clarice's call to 911, and her restraining order. Consequently, after establishing an incredibly lengthy criminal record, the description of Cameron's act of attempted murder sounded quite plausible, so after considering their testimonies, the police closed the case.

Afterward, in an attempt to recuperate from the mental stress of reliving a nightmare, Cory and Clarice spent the next few hours outdoors in the rejuvenating sunshine at Schenley Park. Spending time with nature had a tranquil effect on both of them as they meandered through the park, listening to birds and watching children at play. After a long stroll under the trees, they indulged in a light lunch at the café. After the anxieties they had endured, the carefree afternoon felt more like an upscaled vacation than a casual outing.

Silently thanking God that Clarice was alive and well, Cory leaned across the table and held her hand. "I understand that everything feels hectic right now, but after the holidays, when life resumes a normal routine for both of us, I'd like you to come visit me at the zoo, so we can feed the cubs again. Would you like that?" asked Cory.

Clarice nodded. "Yes, I would enjoy seeing them. I am sure I'll feel better in another month or so. I think working with the cubs would probably be a good form of therapy, extending loving care to sweet creatures who need our attention, instead of sitting home alone self-absorbed. There's no point in that."

Cory smiled, feeling relieved. "I couldn't agree more."

The next morning, the *Pittsburgh Post-Gazette* printed an article which briefly described the unfortunate incident on the Alleghany River, reporting the occurrence as an accidental drowning.

The police withheld statements to the press regarding assault and attempted murder due to what they perceived as Clarice's fragile, emotional state. Cameron's obituary announced the date and time of the funeral service at his boyhood church in his hometown of Connellsville, south of Pittsburgh. After reading the article, Clarice called Cory with the details.

"Cory, would you drive with me to the funeral and stay for the burial? It would help give me some closure," asked Clarice.

"Of course, sweetheart. You know I will," replied Cory.

The following morning after the memorial service, Cory and Clarice stood on a foggy hillside as a metal urn containing Cameron's ashes was buried under a lone elm tree. Beneath Cameron's name, the headstone read simply: "Beloved son—gone too soon." As the other attendees gradually walked away, Cory and Clarice stood a short distance from the gravesite, holding hands in silence. When they were finally alone, Clarice walked up to the tombstone and placed a single, yellow rose in front of it.

Tears in her eyes, she said, quietly and slowly, "Cameron, this is for the love you never found and the life you never knew."

CHAPTER 13

*T*hree days later, Cory called Clarice to see how she was doing. As Cory expected, she still sounded melancholy and withdrawn. Although Cameron's stalking and harassment had ceased, the thought of a life wasted on jealousy and lost needlessly out of spite felt excruciating. Even though Clarice had been liberated from her oppressor, he knew she would need some time for herself after the incident, time to heal emotionally. The last thing she needed was an agonizing memory festering away in her mind like an invisible, gaping wound.

"Cory, I don't want to go out this weekend. It's not you. I don't want to do anything with anyone right now. I just need time to get over Cameron's death and all the trauma he put us through. I'm taking a few days off from work. I really need to sit and work my way through this. I feel tired and numb. I'm sure you understand. Can we aim for next weekend? I would like to see you then."

"We can get together next weekend, if you like. You're going to be okay. Just give yourself some time," said Cory reassuringly.

He fully understood that she needed some time for her bereavement, but that eventually she would find the courage to move forward. Clarice was more than a survivor; she played the role of the leading lady in her own life story and nothing would leave her defeated.

"You're right. Cory, I just can't believe how brave you were, diving in to save me. It's amazing. You showed no fear at all."

"Sweetheart, fear isn't diving off a boat. Fear is owing $200,000 to a guy in Sicily named Antonio who wants all your bones for collateral."

"You always know to make me laugh! Thanks for trying to make me feel better. Oh, Cory, I just want to be happy. Right now, I wish it was Christmas morning. I want to think about the holidays."

She paused a moment to reflect and compose herself.

"Cory, do you think we can spend the holidays together, at least for a few days? You have been so good to me. Let me do something for you. Come with me to visit my parents in Titusville for Christmas. I really want them to meet you. How does that sound?"

Cory smiled. He could not think of anywhere he would rather be than with her during the holidays. She completed him. His life had become a song of joy and success and she was the chorus he wanted to keep singing.

"Ideal. There's someone near there that I want you to meet. A wonderful man who gave me a place to stay when I was traveling to Pittsburgh. Mr. Jamison. You might recall I mentioned him at Thanksgiving. I have only known him a short time, but he feels like a member of the family. I know you are going to like him. He's the man who drove me to the tent revival, the night we met."

"Then I definitely have to meet him in order to thank him for that," Clarice replied warmly.

"Absolutely, sweetheart. I'll call you in a week. We'll make plans then. In the meantime, get some rest and take care of yourself. If you feel like calling me, feel free. Don't hesitate. Bye."

Christmas morning, Clarice and Cory sat in the living room of Mr. and Mrs. Lyons, Clarice's parents. About six inches of snow lay on the ground, making the landscape as picturesque as any greeting card. Cory was greeted like family from the start. As he passed the foyer, he noticed the modern home consisted primarily of an enormous great room, which included the living room, a separate family room, a dining room, and an eat-in kitchen. A nine-foot Christmas tree topped with a Moravian star from Germany stood in the corner to one side of a stone fireplace. The family had meticulously trimmed everything on the main level with holiday decorations.

"Cory, I hope you enjoyed the Christmas service this morning. Pastor Raymond has been with us for ten years and he is passionate about missions," said Clarice's mother.

Cory sat relaxed on the sofa, gazing up at the Christmas tree with his multicolored lights blinking in various patterns. He turned and looked at Clarice's mother. She acted just as charming and graceful as her daughter.

"It was a beautiful service. I especially liked the display of the nativity scene by the altar. His remarks about Christ coming as the Prince of Peace in Luke and the Lion of Judah in Revelation were intriguing. I'm going to have to read more about that later on," said Cory, contemplating where he might find a book on that topic.

"Clarice has told us so much about you that we feel we know you already. We're glad you had the opportunity to visit with her," said Clarice's father.

"I'm glad we made it. Originally, the forecast predicted a blizzard, but for some reason it stayed to the west of us. Erie was hit with several feet of snow, not unusual. We have been talking about coming back to visit in the spring around Easter, if that fits your schedule, of course."

"That would be a good time. We always enjoy a feast at Easter with all the family. We would love for the two of you to join us," said Mrs. Lyons, smiling.

"Cory, these are my brothers, Luke and Phillip. This is my sister, Catherine," said Clarice, gesturing to her siblings.

The two young men looked several years older than Clarice. Her sister, the youngest in the family, was just starting high school. All three of them were quite gregarious, telling Cory about their interests and the last family vacation to the mountains and asking him questions about his job and life in Pittsburgh.

"Cory, I want to show you something," said Clarice, taking Cory gently by the arm.

Clarice walked with him over to the Christmas tree and pointed to a brass bell.

"My great-grandparents owned a farm in the area years ago. Back then, they traveled by horse and buggy or by sleigh in the winter. This bell was on the horse harness they used in winter. When they passed away, everyone wanted the harness, so in an attempt to be fair, my grandfather cut the bells off the harness and distributed them among his kids and grandchildren. This bell is mine. I can tell because I keep mine polished."

She reached up and rang the bell for him.

"What a wonderful keepsake."

Cory began to envision a vacation with Clarice in Vermont at a country inn that offered sleigh rides and other outings.

After an hour of taking turns opening presents around the tree, the family took a break for breakfast.

"We'll finish opening everything after we eat. That's just one of our traditions," Clarice explained.

After a hearty breakfast of waffles, sausage, and eggs, the family resumed their places in the living room to indulge in the pleasure of gift exchange. Cory took out a small box from his jacket pocket and handed it to Clarice.

"This is for you. I hope you like it."

Eagerly opening the box wrapped in red paper, Clarice discovered a porcelain male lion on a golden cord carefully hand-painted to the finest detail.

"Cory, it's lovely. It will look great on the tree. Do you think Justin will look like this when he is full grown?"

"Probably, something like that."

Clarice hung the decoration on the front of the tree and admired it.

"This is something for you," Clarice said smiling, as she reached for a package beneath the tree.

Cory sat down and opened a large box to find a wool, Nordic sweater, red and white.

"Wow, this is beautiful. The wool is extremely soft. This looks like it came from Norway," said Cory, rather astonished.

"It did. I had it shipped from a clothing store in Oslo," said Clarice, smiling.

"Sweetheart, you didn't have to go to so much trouble. That was so thoughtful of you," said Cory, kissing Clarice, who was seated next to him on the sofa.

After an in-depth conversation with Clarice's family, Cory excused himself to make a phone call.

"Paul, it's Cory. I wanted you to know that I am back here in Titusville and would enjoy seeing you, if you're free. I meant to call sooner, but life can get a little hectic."

"Cory, it is so good to hear your voice. I want to know everything that has happened."

For the next ten minutes, Cory provided Paul with the specifics about his job, his new basement apartment, and his relationship with Clarice. Life was turning out perfectly. Paul sat there in the living room listening, delighted at every piece of good news. Cory mentioned nothing concerning the encounters with Clarice's ex-boyfriend. There was no point in spoiling Paul's holiday.

"Let's plan on spending some time together this afternoon and bring Clarice. I would like to meet her."

"She's a terrific gal, Paul. She might be the one. I'll check with her about what the family might have planned. If the afternoon is free, can we come by around two o'clock?"

"Yes, certainly. I'll fix us something hot to drink."

"Thanks, see ya."

Two hours later, Clarice and Cory drove to Paul's cabin just outside of town. As the couple sat on the sofa, Paul prepared his own version of homemade hot chocolate on the stove. After serving the beverage, Paul reclined in the oversized chair by the sofa, resting is boots on the fireplace hearth. The flaming logs radiated plenty of heat. Cory reminisced about the fire he had built the first night he spent at the cabin.

"Mr. Jamison, in all honesty, this is the best hot chocolate I have ever tasted," said Clarice.

"You can call me Paul. I use a secret ingredient: melted Hershey chocolate bars. Combining them with whole milk makes a rich tasting drink."

"It sure does," said Cory, sipping the hot chocolate through the thick layer of whipped cream.

"Cory, how are your parents doing?" asked Mr. Jamison.

"I honestly don't know. I need to phone them today. After all, it is Christmas."

"Have you found a church to attend in Pittsburgh?" asked Mr. Jamison.

"Not yet. Clarice and I were thinking about attending her former church together. She used to live in Pittsburgh and one of the Methodist churches in town was her home church growing up. It sounds like a good place to worship."

Clarice spent the next ten minutes telling Paul about her job and career ambitions. She also described the Christmas ornament Cory had given her and how much she had enjoyed working with the lion cubs.

Taking Clarice by the hand, Cory said, "Paul, would you mind terribly if Clarice and I take a little walk. I'd like to show her the beauty of this place."

"Feel free. It's a gorgeous day."

Clarice and Cory walked out the front of the cabin and down a wooded path. Ice and snow hung from the trees, sparkling in the sunlight. About fifty yards away, they spotted some deer walking through a clearing in the forest.

"Isn't this beautiful? God's outdoor cathedral," said Clarice with a sigh.

Cory put his arm around Clarice as they walked. When they reached the fork in the path, they stopped to admire the spectacular view of the snow covered hills on the horizon. He turned to Clarice and gazed into her eyes a moment, then leaned in slowly for a kiss. He lifted his head and saw her eyes were shut, fully engaged in the moment.

"Clarice, I have something for you."

He took a box out of his pocket.

"Another present? Cory, one was enough."

She unwrapped the box and opened it. Inside something flashed as brightly as the sun on the snow.

"Cory!"

At that same moment, Cory dropped to one knee and reached for Clarice's right hand.

"Clarice, I love you. Will you marry me?"

She let out a shriek of joy, hugged Cory, and kissed him.

"Does that mean 'yes'?"

"Yes! Without a doubt, yes! I love you so much."

"Clarice, I have one more gift for you."

She stared at him in amazement.

Cory took a piece of paper out of his jacket pocket and unfolded it.

"I wrote you a love poem. I think this is the best time to read it to you."

Clarice's eyes got misty as she stood silently and listened.

> *Till time sweeps through my hands on wings anew,*
> *When frozen ground my feet no longer know,*
> *Tis then I'll call my conscience thee to view,*
> *Thy vision of love in spirit to grow.*
> *The clouds they change their form if thou but speak,*
> *A thousand shapes to one accord do join,*
> *As I in hope my head do bow and weep,*
> *For things I seek to give not found with coin.*
> *Thy gaze has fixed my heart in thee to rest,*
> *For fear holds not the door ajar in wait.*
> *Such peace has filled my soul till it is blessed,*
> *As I alone pass through thy garden gate.*
> *Although by space yet still apart we seem,*
> *At one are we for thou art more than dream.*

"Cory, that's beautiful. You wrote that?"

"Yes, sweetheart, for you."

He kissed her and stood there holding her for the longest time.

"Merry Christmas, darling. I love you," Cory said softly.

CHAPTER 14

At five o'clock in the evening, Christmas Day, the Parker's phone rang.

"Mom, it's Cory. How are you?"

His mother let out a shriek of surprise. She had not anticipated Cory's call, although she had hoped and prayed for months that this day would arrive. The sound of his voice pacified her and yet also generated tremendous excitement intermingled with some overtones of regret.

"Cory, we have been so worried about you. Son, before we say another word to each other, your father and I apologize for what we said. We could have been more supportive and understanding."

Turning her head away from the phone, she called out, "Clay, come to the phone. It's Cory." At the sound of his son's name, Mr. Parker leaped out of his chair and ran to the phone. The anxiety over his son's whereabouts for the last three months had become excruciating. How many hours had he sat by the phone hoping Cory would call? How many times had he reprimanded himself for acting more like a dictator than a father? Ever since Cory left, the house seemed lifeless, void of laughter. Now, with his son on the other end of the line, he was not about to inflict any more damage to an already strained relationship. He had always loved his son but somehow his controlling nature had usurped his judgement. It was time to make amends.

"Mom, it worked out for the best. I landed a terrific job that I love and moved in with Carl. You remember Carl. We've been friends forever. And Mom, I met a girl. She's wonderful. I would like for you to meet her."

"Of course, dear. We would love to meet her. Cory, your father's here. He would like to speak with you." Cory's father, almost trembling, took the receiver from his wife's hand. He had missed feeling like a father. Mr. Parker's intense joy combined with a sense of renewal. It was like taking in a breath of fresh air after exiting a smoke-filled room.

"Cory, I am so glad you called. I trust you are doing fine," sounding relieved that the two of them finally reconnected.

"Yeah, Dad. I'm doing great. I have a full-time job that I love, a place to live, and met a fabulous girl." Paternal pride began to swell up inside Mr. Parker. He regretted numerous omissions of guidance and nurturing in Cory's upbringing. Nevertheless, somehow some of his encouragement and sound advice over the years seemed to have been absorbed. Now his son was successful and content with his life. He thought to himself, "*That's my boy!*"

"It doesn't get much better than that. Cory, I am so sorry for yelling at you. I was out of line. Son, these past couple months I've had time to do a lot of thinking. I need to show you the respect you deserve as an adult and I sincerely mean that."

"Thanks, Dad. Apology accepted. I'm sorry too for leaving unannounced and worrying you like I did. Let's just move forward from here." Cory felt elated. At last, the poisonous past was now buried forever like dead snakes in a pit. All vices, including unforgiving natures and contemptuous words, should never be resurrected. The mutual confessions of thoughtless behavior reestablished the long-awaited bond between them.

Meanwhile, Mrs. Parker sat in the living room weeping tears of relief. Cory's phone call equated to the best Christmas present she had ever received. Without Cory, a holiday consisted of one more twenty-four-hour stretch to trudge through like plodding along in knee deep mud after a raging flood. With Cory, the day felt like heaven's rays beamed through every window.

"Yes, good idea. Cory, I want you to know that your mother and I changed churches. We found a fabulous pastor. In fact, your mother and I pray together now every morning. We started praying the day you left. Today our prayers are answered. You called and you're safe."

"Thanks, Dad. My prayers have been answered too. Listen, I'm staying with a friend in Pennsylvania for the holidays, but I plan to come back and visit next week. After all, Christmas is twelve days long, so keep the tree up and we'll celebrate then. How does that sound?"

"That's fine, Cory. I can't tell you how wonderful it is to hear from you. I'm looking forward to your visit."

"Hey, Dad. How's Leo doing?"

"He's fine. He's been sleeping in your room on the rug, since the day you left. He misses you. We all do."

"I miss you guys too. You take care and I'll call again before we leave. I'll be bringing the girl I mentioned and I'll have a surprise for both of you. Bye."

CHAPTER 15

The day after New Year's, Cory and Clarice drove to Chicago, discussing wedding plans along the way. "I hope it won't be any trouble for your parents or friends to attend the wedding in Pittsburgh. It really is such a lovely church. I have such fond memories of attending there as a child. Now, I am going to have the most memorable experience of all," said Clarice, glancing at Cory with an enormous smile. She knew she had found her ideal match and was quite aware that not everyone was that fortunate.

Keeping his eyes on the road, Cory nodded. "It will be the greatest day of my life with the perfect girl. I have never met anyone like you before. You are priceless. Don't worry about the location. Carl is my best friend and he's already there. I have a handful of close friends in Chicago, but they think nothing of taking off on a long drive."

Clarice smiled. "You are different from everyone I've ever met. Most guys announced their plans and acted like I should be grateful to go along for the ride. Know what I mean? They didn't care how I felt and didn't seem to want me as a part of their lives aside from cleaning a house. All they really were after was a live-in maid and cook. When I was twenty, a guy I met at college proposed after two dates. When I asked him why he wanted to get married, he said, 'So someone will take care of me.' Can you believe that? I told him if I got married, I would be someone's wife, not someone's mother. He had no interest in giving, only getting. I never spoke to him again."

"Can't say that I blame you." Cory paused, thinking about the reception. "At some point, let's sit down and make a list of items for the wedding and what things will cost. That way we can try and budget," said Cory, trying to sound practical.

"I'm glad you're frugal." Clarice began again slowly. "Cory, I have good news for you. The lady at the Methodist church who handles receptions, Mrs. Phillips, remembered me from years back. She and my mother remained close all these years. Any rate, Mrs. Phillips has offered to cater the wedding at no cost as long as we can keep the guest list to 75 or less. She wants to do that as our wedding gift. Since neither of us come from huge families, I think we can keep the guest list fairly low. She wants to serve chicken, bread, salad, potatoes, and glazed carrots. She'll even provide the cake, any kind we want. How does all that sound?" asked Clarice.

Cory remained silent a moment, processing one of the best news bulletins he had ever heard. "Clarice, that will save us a fortune! We must have that woman over for dinner to thank her properly. The money saved can go into the house." He sighed with delight. "You're right. We should be able to keep the guest list low in number."

Although it was cold and overcast, surprisingly, the roads were barren with not a hint of snow on the ground, allowing them to arrive sooner than expected.

Upon opening the door, Cory hugged his parents, grateful to feel united with his family again. The long, lost son had returned, but triumphant, a successful man in charge of his destiny.

When Clarice showed her diamond ring to Mr. and Mrs. Parker, they were ecstatic about the engagement. They could not wait to hear all the details of how she had met Cory and their future plans.

Hearing voices at the front door, the German shepherd ran to meet Cory and jumped up on him, his paws landing on Cory's shoulders.

"Leo, buddy. Hey, boy. I sure missed you," said Cory affectionately, while stroking the dog's head and neck.

Cory caressed Leo and then "waltzed" with him around the living room, while Clarice stood there laughing.

That evening, Clarice felt like royalty at a surprise engagement dinner, dining on steak and lobster at one of Chicago's finest restaurants. Mr. Parker could easily see why Cory had chosen Clarice.

"Cory, you picked a real winner. She's a sweet gal with a lovely disposition," Mr. Parker said.

Cory nodded. "Not only that Dad, but she can cook and she's a fantastic dancer," said Cory as he leaned over and kissed Clarice on the cheek.

As Mr. Parker sat there eating dinner and enjoying the company of his family, he noted the enormous change in his son. Cory had found his place in the world, but more importantly, he was willing to help others find theirs. Cory had become self-reliant, confidant, and outspoken, unafraid to speak his mind, while at the same time displaying a sense of selflessness and dedication to the happiness of others. That was evident in the way he interacted with his fiancé.

Likewise, Cory detected a tremendous change in his parents. They extended courtesies to each other that were nonexistent five months ago, as they spoke in calm, benevolent tones. From Cory's perspective, the transformation was complete. Both of his parents cared more about others than themselves. As Cory conversed with them during dinner, he concluded that their reformed natures were nothing short of miraculous.

"Dear, if you need any help financially for the wedding, the reception, the honeymoon, anything at all, you let us know. We will be glad to help out," said Cory's mother, giving him a hug.

"Thanks. Mom, Dad. Clarice and I have talked it over and we want to get married in July at her home church in Pittsburgh, a Methodist church. We'll have a catered reception nearby at a hotel ballroom," said Cory, beaming at his future bride.

"Whatever works out best for the two of you is what is most important. We can make travel arrangements and book a hotel. Don't worry about us," Mr. Parker said emphatically.

That evening, after dinner, while Clarice chatted with her future in-laws, Cory phoned Paul to tell him about the engagement.

"Paul, this is Cory. I have great news. Clarice and I are engaged. I proposed in your back yard at the end of the path, the one I strolled down the same afternoon that I met Clarice. It was the most romantic spot I could find where we could be alone for a few minutes. I didn't tell you right away because I wanted my parents to be the first to know. Of course, you will be invited to the wedding this summer. We hope you'll come."

"Cory, I couldn't be happier for you. I wouldn't miss the wedding for anything," Paul said enthusiastically.

Afterward, he phoned his aunt and cousins to tell them the good news, and then Carl, whom Cory invited to be the best man.

Bursting with enthusiasm, Carl replied, "Cory, that is great news. I would be honored to be best man. I have an idea. How does this sound? As a wedding gift, I will hire one of my photographers for the day to take the wedding pictures. That will be one less thing for you two to worry about."

Cory was speechless. "Carl, I don't know what to say. That is so generous of you. Clarice and I want to celebrate, but we also wanted to consider the cost. We don't want to accrue a massive amount of debt like some couples. A neighbor of ours in Chicago paid over $35,000 for her wedding. I almost passed out from shock, when my mother told me that. Your helping us out is one of the best presents we could get. Clarice will be thrilled when she hears about this."

Finally, he phoned Daniel. "You and your dad are both invited to the wedding. I never would have gotten to Pennsylvania without him," said Cory warmly.

"Cory, my father and I will be there. I know he will be thrilled when I give him the news. I'm so happy for you. God bless you both."

On the return trip to Pittsburgh, the couple began planning where they would live and decided on a location that was a halfway point between each of their places of employment with a back yard, so Leo could romp and enjoy the outdoors. In years to come, the back yard would serve as the playground for their children. Clarice planned to continue working at the newspaper office, while Cory interacted with the cubs. The couple already considered making special trips to the zoo with their future kids to look at all the animals, but especially the lions.

Six months later, everything was ready for the ceremony. As a surprise gift, Daniel had given the couple a large framed picture of the two of them feeding the cubs, which was placed on a reception table in the ballroom of the hotel. This way the lions could in a sense "attend" the wedding. The cubs had played a role in the bonding process of the young couple and both Clarice and Cory had grown to love them dearly.

The wedding chapel looked quite ornate with pink and white flowers interspersed with accents of red. After the flower girl, bridesmaids, and the maid of honor, Clarice's sister, walked down the aisle, the organ played an introduction, and Clarice appeared in the doorway looking regal in her wedding gown with a long train. Cory felt like no other man could ever be as fortunate as he was. As he watched Clarice approach, Cory knew that this was the start of discovering more of the binding ties that unite hearts forever, a lifetime of self-sacrifice, empathy, and trust in God. As each of them made their vows, for a moment they held hands tightly as they both looked up together above the altar at a stained-glass window of a multicolored cross.

At the reception, Cory and Clarice sat at a large table with their closest friends and family. Cory looked over at Paul, Daniel, and his father and marveled that encounters with strangers had enabled him to reunite with his best friend and discover his true love. As Cory watched his parents enjoying dinner and conversing with guests, he realized that he had learned to relinquish the past and forgive the transgressions of others as well as his own failures and shortcomings. He had acquired the skill of embracing life to the fullest. Most importantly, he had allowed life to embrace him. As Cory held Clarice's hand, he realized that God had set him up to succeed, not only by introducing him to the love of his life, but also by teaching him that genuine success is not measured in financial security, but rather in the desire to love and empower others, a lesson in wisdom and grace he had learned from embracing Christ, the Lion of Judah.

About the Author

Cynthia J. Sebring, the author of the novel *Guardian of the Dove*, became a writer after thirty-two years in the field of education. Over the course of her career, she served on numerous committees and advisory boards, including the Superintendent Teacher Advisory Council (STAC). She is a two-time recipient of the Congressional Youth Leadership Council Award.

As a graduate student of English, Ms. Sebring focused her studies primarily on literature, literary analysis, and the creative writing process. As part of her undergraduate program, the author spent a summer abroad studying German literature and language acquisition at the University of Trier. Ms. Sebring has traveled extensively throughout Europe, the United States, and Canada, and she frequently uses these experiences as sources of inspiration for her novels.

The author has earned master's degrees from the following institutions of higher learning:

MA Theology, Christendom College, Front Royal, VA
MA English, George Mason University, Fairfax, VA
MA Education, University of Phoenix, Phoenix, AZ